The Steel Web

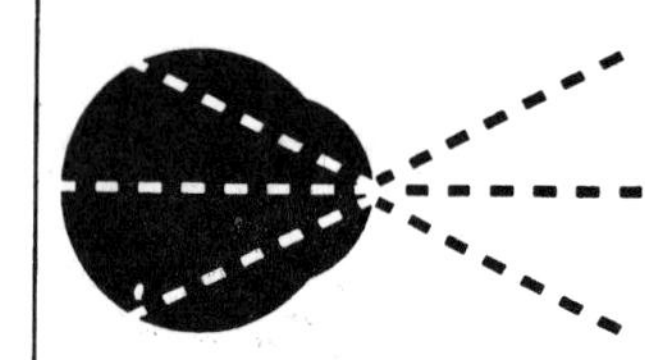

This Large Print Book carries the Seal of Approval of N.A.V.H.

The Steel Web

Ronald Tierney

G.K. Hall & Co.
Thorndike, Maine

Published in Large Print by arrangement with
St. Martin's Press.

G.K. Hall Large Print Book Series.

Printed on acid free paper in the United States of America.

Set in 18 pt. Plantin.

Library of Congress Cataloging-in-Publication Data

Tierney, Ronald.
The steel web / Ronald Tierney.
p. cm. —(G.K. Hall large print book series)
ISBN 0-8161-5458-9
1. Large type books. I. Title.
[PS3570.I3325S69 1993]
813'.54—dc20 92-40636

To Frances Ruth Tierney and
J. Gregory Tierney

"You have no idea what it's like to live with a man who never laughs."

—LENORA CONNELL

ONE

"What I'm trying to tell you is that I'm leaving town," Shanahan said into the black rotary-dial telephone. "Tomorrow."

Shanahan sat at his desk in his living room, looking at the faded floral print of the wallpaper his first wife put up thirty-five years ago, two months before she skipped town. He never liked it. Not then. Not now. And he didn't like Mrs. Dunfy, who wanted to hire him to snoop on her husband. He held the phone away from his ear as the woman spoke.

"I don't do divorce work," he said quickly when she finally took a breath. He looked at the papers on his desk, the torn envelope from his Social Security check used as a bookmark for his girlfriend's paperback novel.

"I'm gonna be gone for two weeks." He thought about the expenses a trip like Hawaii would set him back. He didn't want to go, but Maureen did. And in a weak moment, a very weak moment, he had said he would, so he would.

"Get off!" Shanahan yelled. "No, not you, Mrs. Dunfy, my cat." Einstein, who looked like and was about half the size of a raccoon, liked to be between wherever Shanahan was and where he was looking.

"Why'd you choose me anyway? Yes, now I'm talking to you, Mrs. Dunfy . . . I'll call you when I get back. If you still want your husband investigated and you haven't found anybody else, I'll take it. Good-bye."

He hung up the phone, brushed Einstein off the edge of the desk and into the path of Casey, Shanahan's dog, who nipped playfully at the cat's tail. Einstein turned and gave the dog a swift uppercut, walking away with a small amount of his pride restored.

"Why'd she chose you?" Maureen asked.

"Because she's sure no one has ever heard of me."

The two sixteen-year-olds never got much. Maybe a portable TV. A Walkman or a ghetto blaster if they were lucky.

Leo and Billy had staked out the place for a solid week. The guy who lived there left five minutes ago, just like he always did, heading down Washington Street toward the Taco Bell, a copy of *The Indianapolis Star* tucked under his arm. But he couldn't have. Something had gone wrong. Very wrong. The guy wasn't sitting down the street munching on a beef burrito. He was flat out on the floor with a bayonet sticking in his ribs.

"You ever see so much blood?" Leo said, staring around the room, mouth gaping.

"I say we get out of here," Billy said, using his hand to sweep back the lock of brown hair that slipped back down over his eyes immediately.

Leo was on his knees. Carefully, he slid his hand into the dark charcoal suit jacket, inside the breast pocket, trying to avoid touching the bayonet sticking out of the black guy's chest and trying not to touch the blood all over the guy's shirt. Out came a thick wallet. Deftly, despite the fact that his nails were bitten to the quick, the blond-haired kid fanned the crisp stack of bills.

"Hundreds," Leo said, "maybe fifty of 'em." His eyes sparkled.

"All right," Billy said slowly, "put five of them back." He was already by the window. His look was somber.

"What! You crazy?"

"I say we get out of here. You know. Like we were never here. Put five hundred back in the wallet and put it back—exactly where you found it."

"What are you talking about, Billy?"

"A man's got money in his wallet, nobody says robbery. Right? So why would we kill the fucker?"

"But five of them? C'mon, Billy."

Billy gave him the look, the look he always gave when he thought Leo was being stupid or acting too crazy.

"Yeah, okay. I got it," Leo said. He did what he was told.

Outside, walking back, Billy said, "Shit. How we gonna unload hundreds?"

"You're always looking on the bad side. Five thousand bucks, Billy. We'll find a way."

"Don't tell Lisa," Billy said. He looked around. Everything seemed pretty normal. They passed a couple of empty storefronts with dirty windows and a car lot, soapy numbers on the windshields. Leo's eyes inventoried the autos.

"You always gotta have secrets, Billy."

"Yeah, well, in case you forgot already, there's a dead man in there, and the more people that know we were there . . ."

"Okay, okay. Look at that red Camaro. Cherry." Already Leo's mind darted to new thoughts.

"Don't get any ideas. We start flashing this shit around and pretty soon some goon gonna say, where'd these punks get the bread."

"We're not punks, and anyway, nobody knows us from shit, Billy. Nobody gives a shit."

"We don't spend any of this till we have a chance to think about it, all right?"

"That's you, Billy. Thinkin' and worryin' about things. Don't you ever do nothin'?"

Billy smiled, tossed his head once again to get the hair out of his eyes. Didn't say anything.

Hawaii was the last place he ever wanted to go. Now he was happy. Shanahan had just spent twenty minutes letting the surf twist his sixty-nine-year-old body into a soggy pretzel. He was just learning to catch the wave to body surf in when he felt his body just give up.

On the beach were two kids with short sunboards that looked like they were made of Styrofoam. They wore knee-length shorts in Day-Glo colors, one orange, the other green. Young, tan, healthy and happy, they stared at Shanahan as if he were the Loch Ness monster; the old man was breathing so heavy and coughing saltwater out of his nostrils, they must have thought he was going to die.

"The water's fine," Shanahan said, "try it."

The kids giggled.

He was content to lie back on his towel, breathe heavily and watch Maureen romp the long stretch of Makena beach in Maui. She ran in and out of the water, looking more like eighteen than forty-five. Of course, he didn't deserve her. What good thing had he done in his life to have a happy, intelligent, fun-loving woman want to share her life with him?

Shanahan watched as she approached, shaking the water from her reddish-brown hair.

"You did pretty good. Sometimes I saw your head, sometimes your legs. Pretty funny." She grinned, kissed him on the cheek. "You ready for a surfboard, Frankie, or should I say, Mr. Avalon?"

"Call me Kahuna. Big Kahuna, to you."

"All right, Mr. Kahuna. There's another beach just over that big rock."

"What's wrong with this one?"

"People are wearing swimming suits here," she said, raising her eyebrows.

"And over there they're wearing dinner jackets?"

They made the trek toward the rock that separated the two beaches. They climbed. There was a sign posted at the top that said NUDITY PROHIBITED. The word "prohibited" had been sprayed over, and the word "required" replaced it.

Shanahan felt better when he noticed that the beach was small and sparsely populated. There was an older man with a beard, sitting in a lawn chair, accompanied by his dog. There was another guy, a fortyish body-beautiful type, stretched spread-eagle on a perfectly smooth sheet. A couple of guys in their early twenties sitting with pretty, well-tanned girlfriends, drinking Coronas.

Somebody was trying to get a volleyball game going, and an Irish setter was being given a workout by a couple of athletic-looking guys with a Frisbee. Shanahan wished he looked as good and moved as well.

Maureen took off her halter top, and Shanahan found he was the only one who paid any attention to her lack of modesty.

He smiled, took a deep breath and opened a musty Erskine Caldwell novel. He hadn't read a novel in twenty years. He had found this among the books left by his first wife when she deserted him for her hairdresser and moved to Arizona. That was even more years ago. She was Maureen's age then.

Shanahan had met Maureen at a massage parlor west of town, invited her to dinner. One thing led to another. That was six months ago. She quit her job, moved in.

"You're not going to get naked with me?" Maureen asked.

Shanahan put on his reading glasses, gave her body a complete appraisal. "Not here. Besides, I'd rather see than be seen."

"Hunks," she said, glancing toward the Frisbee players.

"Yep."

"You ever look like that?"

"Nope."

"Good," she said, rubbing his chest. "Pretty, but not sexy."

"Me?" He lowered his drugstore cosmetic-counter glasses, looking out at the bronzed muscular bodies.

"No, them."

"Oh."

"They're probably in love with themselves or with each other."

"Well, I wish them every happiness, whatever it is."

"Me too. And us too. Follow me," she said, getting up, grabbing her suit top and racing down the beach. Shanahan got up, but he really wasn't in the mood to play eighteen again. He walked quickly instead, watching her disappear off to the right, taking a sandy path that led into underbrush, which soon turned into overbrush.

He had to duck tree limbs, keep from tripping over roots in the well-worn path. The trail twisted and turned and occasionally forked. Shanahan had no idea which way she'd gone but continued to follow the most beaten of the paths.

It led up. Ever so slightly at first, then getting rockier and steeper. He found himself out from under the trees now, feet burning on the white rock that seemed to have been strewn in anger. His soles hurt from the jagged edges.

Shanahan had veered right, and apparently Maureen had veered left. He could see her, down on the other side of the rocks, running into more trees, her auburn hair floating behind her like that of a goddess.

He told himself he was a mountain goat, and stepped carefully until he had gotten over the rocks and could now walk on smooth ground toward the large clump of trees.

She was there. She was laughing, catching her breath. She untied her bikini bottom.

Something puzzled Shanahan. When they got back from the beach, Maureen was happy. She was even teasing him about a little sex in the afternoon.

"Again?" he'd asked.

"It's the sun," she'd declared, smiling.

However, when Shanahan came out of the shower, she was quiet. Different. Distant.

On the cool drive into Lahaina, the ocean and sunset off to the left, he let her be. She stared off into it, but Shanahan was pretty sure she wasn't admiring the view. At Longhi's, the restaurant she had chosen and was so excited about going to, she sipped her Margarita, played listlessly with her pasta.

He looked across the table. She was beautiful. He loved it when she didn't wear makeup, when she had her hair down, when she wore her khaki pants and white shirt open at the neck so he could see the light freckles that dotted her chest.

"Not happy," he said to her.

"I've made reservations to fly back tomorrow," she said, still looking down at her food.

"I was in the shower maybe twenty minutes. What happened in twenty minutes?"

"I went over to the main house. There was an express letter." She spoke without emotion, a coolness he'd rarely seen in her. "Dad's dying," she said, as if she were telling him she needed dishwashing liquid from the store.

"When do we leave?"

"You don't have to leave. Stay here. You can't do anything."

"I can be there."

"I've been thinking, Shanahan. I don't think I want you there. It's something I have to do by myself."

"Well, I'm going back with you, just in case."

The flight was endless. They were routed through Chicago and it took forever to land, forever at the terminal, and forever getting clearance to take off for Indianapolis.

There was only a little light left, but Shanahan could make out the patchwork land below, various shades of brown squares interrupted occasionally by a river or a small gathering of buildings. From what he could see, the rivers were brown and the trees either deep red or yellow, some looking like gray lace where the leaves had already fallen.

Once home, Maureen packed a few things and left immediately. The house seemed sad and empty. Hours ago they were in the sun, lush greens, blue sky. But now Shanahan's environment seemed to mirror the sudden change in reality. Outside, the sky was gray, and inside, the house looked forlorn, sad. He hadn't done anything to it since his wife left, too many years ago to count, and Maureen had made no attempt to make a mark. He had been thankful for that. Now he wasn't so sure.

Shanahan played back the answering machine. One message in three days—from a Mrs. Dunfy. She left her number.

Two

What the lady told him to do was follow the guy. Night-shift work. Parking outside of apartment buildings, restaurants. It was cold, goddammit—not as bad as it would get—but too cold for Dietrich Shanahan. "Deets" his friends called him—a sixty-nine-year-old, German-Irish former Army Intelligence sergeant who supplemented his Army retirement and token Social Security payments with a few odd assignments.

But what the hell, Shanahan told himself when the lady wanted to hire him. Maureen was going to be out of town for a while. He was bored, and the Cubs weren't going to be in the playoffs this year.

Three hours he sat in his green 1972 Chevy Malibu waiting for Mrs. Dunfy's husband to come out. All he observed was the lights in apartment 207 go on, then off then on again. At 10:59 P.M., when the lights came on, Shanahan counted to sixty and headed toward the building. He caught the door as Dunfy, trying to button his

Burberry raincoat, made his way to a shiny pearl-black Acura Legend. Shanahan didn't need the license plate number. He knew who owned the car.

Robert Dunfy—a psychologist who operated a stress clinic, held seminars, and wrote best-selling self-help books—was having an affair, the wife said. "I think it's homosexual," Mrs. Dunfy had told him smugly. Shanahan wondered what the wife would think when she found out who her balding, black-bearded husband was playing around with. What met Shanahan at the door of number 207 was something else altogether—about seventeen, long golden hair and pouty lips.

"Robert . . ." she said breathlessly, flinging open the door and obviously thinking the successful Robert Dunfy had forgotten something. "Who are you?"

Shanahan feigned a mild case of elderly confusion, apologized and said he'd gotten the wrong door. Out of habit, he checked the name on the mailbox below as he left. "S. Granelli."

The guy sure knew how to reduce stress and make the most of it, Shanahan thought. Different worlds. He was sorry the case was over so quickly.

At the bar, Shanahan walked in to find the regulars. Harry, Shanahan's best friend—a guy he had known since World War Two—was entertaining the group with another one of his stories.

"Hi, Deets," Delaney, the balding bartending proprietor, said, automatically bringing Shanahan the long-necked, clear bottle of Miller's. "Long time . . ."

"Yeah."

"Well, lookee here," Harry said. "If it isn't Dietrich Shanahan walking around on two legs like he's still among the living. So the lovely Maureen let you out, did she?"

"Shame they let you out at all," Shanahan told him.

Harry laughed and punched Shanahan on the shoulder. "My treat." He shoved a five at Delaney. "Deets, you look like a man who could take a shot with that beer."

Delaney poured a jigger of J.W. Dant and set it down in front of Shanahan, who looked at it for a moment before he drained it.

"No kiddin', Deets, you always get scarce when you got a woman."

"It happens so often."

"Well, it was that way with what's-her-name in France."

"Harry, you're talking like Paris was last week. That was in 1944, almost half a century ago. Besides, there's only been three women in my life. How many you fallen for?"

"There's only been one woman in my life," Harry said, trying to look serious.

"The one you're with now. How's the song go?"

"You already said it. 'Love the one you're with.' " Harry grinned. "Spot him another bourbon, Delaney. 'Tis a mortal crime, a man his age has got a pretty, young girlfriend and still he has sorrow written all over him."

Because Shanahan had a garden, and because he was a miserable housekeeper, he also had a rich assortment of insects. Moths of every color, beetles of every size and complexion, and spiders: big black ones with hairy legs, tall thin ones with spindly legs, and tiny albino types that looked like flecks of dry skin.

Intrigued by the night lights or preparing for harder, colder times, these creatures found their way into his house. He could see them in the dim light from the desk lamp. The yellowish moonlike illumination fell softly on the sofa, where he sat—another night alone. He'd been through years of these kinds of nights. But not lately. And it was damn hard to get used to again.

It wasn't fair. A few days ago he was in Hawaii with Maureen for what was supposed to be a honeymoon of sorts. Neither wanted to bother with the marriage, but they were living together. Three days in a little cabin on Malea Bay in Maui. Maureen found the place, a cozy, one-room guest house with a large window and a private beach the size of an average living room. The size didn't matter.

In the morning the sun rose large over the mountain on the other side of the bay, and in the evening the moon came up in nearly the same place. In the early mornings, Shanahan went down to the beach and followed the little white crablike creatures, almost transparent as they scampered across the light-soaked sand. In the evening there were black crablike creatures who edged over the black lava rocks. Were they the same? White for morning, black for evening? Probably not, but nature could be like that.

Though he'd never tell a soul, Shanahan

had never believed humans were a superior species. Each species had its own kind of intelligence—none better than the other, only different.

He thought of Casey, his dog. That dog had a brain that could obviously catalog innumerable smells. He knew whether it was a stranger or friend before they came to the door. He could track his beloved tennis ball in a blizzard, nose to the ground, tracing the object by following some pattern that seemed convoluted to Shanahan, and ending up with it in his mouth.

Shanahan could even hide the ball, out of sight, high on a windowsill or something, and Casey would get to the point and look up barking, demanding the prized possession be returned or, better yet, thrown. But no human could use the sense of smell in that way.

He remembered reading about the strange species of lightning bug that could counterfeit the light pattern of the other species. It was the female altering the little blinks of yellow light to attract a male not of her kind. She invited him to dinner—rather, invited him to become dinner, the way a praying mantis and some spiders who devour their mates do.

What a beautiful place, Maui. Orange butterflies. Trees with electric-blue flowers. Rocks with green lichens. All of nature seemed to be charged with a powerful, inner energy. So too was he. Alive and happy.

Eleven heavenly days left. They seemed an eternity still. And Maureen gets a Federal Express letter telling her to come home. Death. He couldn't escape it. It hunted him down. So far, it was always somebody else's. Then again, nearing seventy himself, he was well aware of it in the offing.

Shanahan looked around. Relics of long-separated, but recently dead, wife commingled with a smattering of Maureen's more recent artifacts. There was a picture of Maureen's son. There was the book she finished the first day on the beach. Next to it were real estate study books. Maureen had decided to become a real estate agent—a pretty ambitious move for a forty-five-year-old woman who had spent the last few years working in a massage parlor.

Shanahan dismissed the idea of going to the kitchen for a little more J.W. Dant, even though it might help him sleep. What would he do tomorrow? Tracking down wayward husbands wasn't his idea of a good time, but it helped him fill a few hours. Now it was over. He needed something to keep him busy. The garden wouldn't demand much now. Winter was ahead.

Shanahan flipped on the TV. The gray-green light gave the living room an unnatural color. He'd call the lady with the wayward husband in the morning. No, he'd better stop by, tell her in person.

He glanced at the TV. A man with curly white hair stared back out through the little electronic window. ". . . Storm warnings for a band stretching from the south, including Bloomington, to the north, including Muncie. The warning is in effect for residents of Indianapolis and Marion County until midnight . . ." the man said.

Shanahan fixed himself a bowl of popcorn, changed his mind again and poured himself a glass of J.W. Dant bourbon and watched a Jack Benny rerun. By the time reruns of *Moonlighting* came on, he had gratefully given in to sleep and was adrift on his lumpy sofa. He hated that show. "Too cute," he told Maureen one day. He didn't like detective books or detective shows, except maybe *The Rockford Files*.

When the rains came at midnight, they came violently and imprisoned Billy, Leo, and—much to Billy's displeasure—Lisa, in the only habitable room of the boarded-up house on Dearborn.

Leo appeared to be the tougher of the two. At seventeen, he'd filled out a little. Still lean, he nonetheless carried about twenty more pounds than Billy. He was also the more outgoing of the two, a con artist even his victims found hard to dislike. He had a girl. Lisa. She didn't exactly live there. But she might as well have.

Leo sat on the bed in his jockey shorts, Lisa beside him, watching Johnny Carson. Billy sat under the lamp on a pillow reading an *X-Men* comic book. The electricity came from several connected extension cords that ran out of the second-story window, through a pile of trash, and into the garage of the house next door. The neighbors never noticed the increase in their electric bill; but then again, how much current can you use on one line, even with a four-way socket?

"No, Leo, dammit, I said no," Lisa said. She tried to push his hands away.

"C'mon, Lisa . . . be a sport huh?" Leo had hold of the back of her brunette head, pulling it to his lap.

"Not now, damn you," she said, her voice somewhere between tough and tears. She pulled free, nodded toward Billy, then gave Leo her most serious look.

Leo was on his third wine cooler. He'd convinced Billy they could break one of the hundreds at the liquor store. That old man Price wouldn't give a shit. Leo took a swig, then renewed his attack.

"I mean it, Leo. Not now . . ." she whined.

"You mean Billy? He don't care," Leo said, pressing his nose against hers. "Billy's my friend, ain't you, Billy?"

Billy didn't answer. Usually when Leo got horny, he and Lisa would wait until Billy crashed. Even though they all shared the same bed, Lisa figured it was all right if Billy was asleep. Only usually he wasn't. And he'd feel the bed bounce and he'd hear the sounds. Or sometimes Billy'd go for a walk, but he wasn't fuckin' goin' for a walk in this storm.

"We can wait, Leo," she said. "You know I want to, but not now, okay, Leo?" Her voice whined at an even higher pitch. Billy's shoulders shook at the sound of her voice, "Okay, Leo!"

"I know you want to. Fact is I can't keep you off me most of the time. Now c'mon, Lisa." He reached up, caught her head, brought it down to his lap.

Billy looked up over his comic book, curious. Who was going to win? Leo would. In the end, Lisa could never say no. Then, all of a sudden, she wasn't in a position to say anything. Lisa looked over at Billy and shrugged. Billy pushed the hair back from his eyes and went back to the comic book.

"See, I told you Billy wouldn't mind," Leo said, lying back, laughing.

Edie Porter hated mornings. She'd hate them more as winter approached, when she'd have to get up in the dark. Upshank Manufacturing was half an hour away, across town. In a month or two it'd not only be dark, but cold. She would have to get up fifteen minutes early to warm up the Datsun, to scrape the ice from the windshield and pull out of the driveway by six-fifteen, to be at the plant by seven.

Then, what she'd do all day was sit on a metal chair on a cold concrete floor in front of this huge piece of machinery—a punch press—and turn small, flat brass plates into some sort of brass cup used in plumbing. She didn't know exactly how the piece was used. All she knew is that she was expected to turn out four hundred or so during her regular shift.

She'd been at Upshank for two years, a little more actually, and she didn't like the idea. She'd had two choices. She could have taken this job, or she could have danced at a strip bar on Pendleton Pike on the northeast side.

Edie had even auditioned a couple of months earlier, got a job, worked one week, and knew working days at the factory and nights at the club wasn't going to work out. She didn't mind taking her clothes off that much, and she'd met a couple of guys, one of whom she still saw, but she knew she wasn't bold enough to get the kind of tips that would make a difference. And she was pretty sure the goofy manager was going to give her the boot anyway. So she quit.

Edie wasn't exactly living out her dream, the one she'd had in Bedford, Indiana, about the big city. Maybe it would have been worse if she'd moved to Chicago. Chicago was tougher than Indy, wasn't it?

Sitting in the cold factory, hospital-green

walls, old punch presses of varying vintages lined up in rows with paint peeling off them and people walking around without fingers, she wasn't sure she wouldn't have been happier doing a little bump and grind. In four hours she'd go to the lunchroom, a room with picnic tables and vending machines, and have a half-hour of fantasy, the halfway point in her eight-hour day.

Every morning James A. Connell took inventory. Who and where he was in life was very important. And in his mind it was also measurable. A graduate of Yale, owner of Connell, Baines and Hollyfield, the city's largest locally owned brokerage firm; co-owner of two construction companies; the major shareholder in a corporation that owned and managed twenty-five health complexes for senior citizens. Connell would rate more than a paragraph in anybody's Who's Who.

He was on the board of one of the country's largest pharmaceutical firms, a bank, an insurance company. His power, his presence, extended beyond Indianapolis. He served on three presidential commissions, so many governors' task forces he couldn't name them all. He had been invited to dinner at the White House three times, one each under Nixon, Kennedy, and Carter; and he'd had lunch twice with young Danny Quayle—once before and once after the ascension.

Sure he had inherited his money and to some extent his power, but he'd achieved the rank of colonel in the Marines. And when he got out at forty-two, he went after and got his law degree.

This morning he went into his wife's bedroom, as he always did before leaving, to kiss her good-bye, usually on the forehead. She seldom stirred. It didn't matter. It didn't matter that they weren't close anymore. She had her life. He had his. They considered divorce eight years ago, but neither of them saw any point to it. Just fertile ground for gossip, and it would make life difficult for the kids. And what? Would he give up the life he led now to be with some sex-charged bimbo? And, of course, that's what attracted him. He might choose to live a bit on the edge, but he wasn't a fool, he told himself.

At fifty-five, Connell had had his affairs. He was in the midst of one now, though he was sure Lenora didn't know about this one, as she knew of some of his past dalliances. It was acceptable. Most of the people he knew, those who shared directorships and presidential appointments, did the same thing. Even his two sons, now out of the house and roughly on their own, knew he fooled around. They accepted it, accepted it far better than they would a divorce. It was the way a man lived. Only his daughter didn't know. She was now away at Georgetown.

He stopped at the doorway, looked at his wife again. She was a tough woman. In many ways tougher than he was, the kind of woman who knew what she wanted and got it, save maybe his fidelity.

James A. Connell went down the huge, curved staircase on his way to the kitchen. The place seemed like a hotel to him. It always had. Even when it was his father's house. But it seemed even more so now after Lenora had it redone by some local light of an interior decorator—designer, they're called now. He couldn't remember the name. Only the pink, scrubbed face with gray hair and a gray sweater and gray shoes.

In the kitchen Maribel had the coffee ready. And the toast. Plain toast, no butter. Few of the people he knew at his age could still get in their military uniforms. He could.

He got into his white Mercedes. He didn't know shit about classical music, but his daughter had given him a CD—Bach—and Connell found he liked it. It got his mind clicking. The car glided down the blacktop, taking the curves with grace. He would surprise them at the magazine. He'd bought the little city publication five years ago on a lark and had almost forgotten about it. Today, he was glad he had.

This was the best part of the morning, passing through the long green lawn, the ancient fir trees. He had once toyed with the idea of cutting them down so that his lawn would look more like a golf course, but Lenora looked at him in the most serious way. "You touch those trees, Jim," she said, "and you're a dead man." He was glad now that he didn't. Golf was an old man's game.

He punched the little plastic box and the iron gate slid to the side.

He was back in the world he didn't completely control, and there was always that slight tinge of anxiety as he swung into the street. "No need to worry," he said to himself. He was sure things would work out, things would come out well. They always had.

Shanahan's morning was not a good one. He'd gotten used to sleeping with someone again. Difficult at first, but now it seemed essential. He had been restless.

It must have been Maureen going to see her father that made him dream what he did. His own father, sitting out on the front lawn in Albion, Wisconsin, watering the lawn, the white frame house always meticulously painted behind him. It was the only time he saw his father at rest, at peace with himself, sitting in the white Adirondack lawn chair on the well-manicured grass, making a stream of water arch, dance, and seemingly promenade gracefully over the green carpet. His father died at sixty-three. Shanahan was already six years past his father's exit. Yet his father seemed older than Shanahan, far older.

That was it. A simple dream.

But it made Shanahan think of those summers that seemed to stretch out forever, made him think of peonies, and purple-bearded irises and white roses, all of which his mother nurtured. The fresh tomatoes, lemonade, squeezed from dozens of lemons, let sit out the night before drinking.

Shanahan had been reared well. He had gone proudly into the Army, sent off by friends and relatives gathered in the backyard, toasted by his father, who raised his glass of lemonade for the crowd to follow.

He wondered what kind of life Maureen had had growing up. She hadn't said much. But there were faint allusions to her parents, generally happy when she talked of her mother, generally not when her father was mentioned. Then she would change the subject.

Yet he grew into an old grouch, and Maureen was nearly always happy.

During the night Einstein had caught a mouse. Not uncommon, and it would grow more common as it grew cooler. Maureen had not yet witnessed the results of Einstein's midnight-to-dusk prowl, a grisly corpse and obviously not quickly killed.

That was the most unlikable part of a cat's character, that desire to play with the kill, as if it was just too much fun to have it end quickly.

He got a paper towel, picked the dead,

wet, furry corpse up by the tail, took it to the toilet and flushed.

Shanahan went outside rather than feed the cat, a sort of admonition to his cohabitant of ten years not to do those things, knowing full well no connection in Einstein's brain was made to the murder and the postponement of breakfast.

He stared for a moment at his apple tree. One of the two main limbs that were left had borne no apples this last spring and had only a few leaves. He was sure the tree would be down to half by the time winter was over. He had planted it when he and his wife moved in, shortly after the war. He had nearly seen the cycle. Nature, that entity everyone was always trying to get back to, was a bitch.

He puttered with the screens, taking them out and putting them in the garage, and replacing them with storm windows. Shanahan thought about washing them first. His father would have been horrified that he decided he could get by without doing it.

He threw the tennis ball for Casey, though neither one of them seemed particularly excited by the idea. Casey returned the ball dutifully, but his sad eyes seemed to ask: “Must we?” The ground was too muddy, and Casey wasn’t much for the elements.

Back inside, Shanahan brushed Einstein off the counter. “This is mine,” he told the feline as he went back to slicing green olives for his cream cheese sandwich. “Don’t you ever leave the kitchen?” The cat hopped back up, but stayed his distance, staring at the cream cheese. “Here, try an olive.” Einstein sniffed once, jerking back as if he’d been slapped. Shanahan scooped up a bit of the cheese on his finger and put it on the counter in front of the cat. “You should have to eat brussels sprouts. I do.”

Shanahan looked out the kitchen window. Casey was being bawled out by an angry squirrel.

After demolishing the cream cheese, Einstein gave his benefactor’s forearm a nudge, a ritual Shanahan took as a show of gratitude. “You’re welcome.”

“Who the hell are you talking to?” came a deep voice.

Shanahan pivoted to see the hulking figure and bearded face of Lieutenant Rafferty, a police officer for whom he felt little respect.

"Sorry Shanahan. Don't have a coronary on me. I need you."

"You know, out there on the door, is a doorbell. You know why people put doorbells on their doors?"

"C'mon, I thought we made up, eh?"

"No, no. All we did was agree not to kill one another. As far as I'm concerned, we didn't even agree to be civil. So why don't you leave as quietly as you came in?" Shanahan bit into his sandwich.

"Looks good," Rafferty said, sitting down at the Formica table. "Why don't you make me one of those?"

"What do you want, Rafferty? Is this official?"

"Sort of. Official for you. Unofficial for me. About the sandwich, though, it's official. I'm starved."

"Let's get past your considerable appetite for a minute and get to the point." Shanahan glared at the corpulent police lieutenant who had a penchant for fine food, fine clothes, and not-so-fine women.

"Money. If you're not going to feed me," Rafferty said, shoving the other chair away from the table with his foot, "at least sit down and hear me out. I want to avail myself of your services, Mr. Detective."

THREE

"How are you?" Shanahan asked, cupping the phone to his ear.

"Holding up," Maureen said before a long pause.

"Your father?"

"The same." Again there was a pause. It seemed awkward.

"Are you tired?" he asked, trying to figure out what was wrong with her voice.

"No," she said.

"Have I called you at an inconvenient time?"

"No, there's just nothing to say."

"How about I come down—be with you?"

She said no too quickly, then tried to be casual. "There's nothing for you to do here. It would only mean there would be two . . . there are things up there, I'm sure."

"Yes, all right," Shanahan said, not wanting to go further into the meaning of "there would be two . . ." Two what? "You still love me?" he asked. It was her phrase and he tried to make a joke of it.

"We'll talk later," she said. "I've got to go."

The leaves were still dripping when Shanahan went into the garden. He looked at the huge trees planted forty years ago, when the homes were built, when everything and everyone seemed fresh and young.

He had wanted to tell Maureen about the case. About Rafferty hiring him to investigate some strange murder on the Eastside, to free a couple of kids Rafferty said the prosecutor was going to fry because it was election year. However, Maureen didn't seem interested.

The two of them had a great summer, he and Maureen. They worked in the garden. Maureen proved to be handy with pruning shears and wasn't afraid of hard work or getting her hands dirty.

They thinned out the irises and created a whole new bed for them in the front. They spent a weekend in New York celebrating the bonus he received from his last client, who hired him to find a missing husband, then kept him on to clear her of his murder. A good deed, some welcome cash—no doubt he was happier than he'd been in decades. Those were three wonderful days in Maui. Then the curtain came down.

It seemed, though, that the first cold wind of fall brought with it another kind of chill. When Maureen was called to her father's bedside—during those hours before she left—she remained cold, distant. He could feel it on the plane and he couldn't look at her. Instead, he'd looked down at the quilted farmlands below, earth that had spent its greenery, preparing itself for a desolate winter. And now the phone call—polite, but terse. Anxiety? Perhaps. But so cold.

No, he knew. It was the inevitable comparison of her father to him. He was sure it was a drama that was playing out as a prologue to the day when he himself would die. She was too bright not to see it.

Shanahan pulled a small apple-tree limb to the pile of dead branches at the back of the yard. Casey followed, a soiled green tennis ball in his mouth. On the way back to the house Shanahan took the ball and tossed it high into the air. Casey moved across the lawn, looking up. He stopped underneath, waited, caught it effortlessly.

"That's pretty good, Case."

He tossed another, straight up. He watched the ball descend through the trees. The leaves hadn't yet changed color. Some autumns it was grand. Sometimes not. The seasons seemed all screwed up. There was maybe one spring in the last five that lived up to the ones he remembered as a young man—one spring that didn't have a false start and then a freeze, waiting until the buds came out, then icing them down.

The tennis ball hit the ground and struck a rock, careening over the fence into the neighbor's yard. Casey stared through the fence for a few moments, then back at Shanahan.

Though Shanahan recognized his neighbors when he saw them, he didn't know them. None of them. How many years can you live someplace and not know your neighbors?

"I'll get a new one," he said, heading toward the house. But the thought reminded him of how reclusive he'd been since his wife had left him, and how long he'd lived with just the idle chatter at Delaney's bar to keep him in touch with the living; a tenuous link, considering the clientele.

Maureen had brought him back to life.

"English!" the voice rang through the office. The voice belonged to James A. Connell, who was only incidentally the publisher, a usually absent publisher who normally tended to his brokerage business, or his construction business, but who this very morning claimed his—up to this point honorary—role as publisher, and who usurped immediately Sarah Mundy's editor-in-chiefship because, as he told her, he "damn well felt like it."

Sarah Mundy flinched, tightened her lips at the second breach in the agreement Connell had reached with her when she became editor. "Tom," she said to the reporter who bore the fateful last name of English, "go on."

He gave her an "I had nothing to do with it" look.

"I know," she said. She took off her glasses and ran her hand back across her short-cropped gray hair. "Do what he wants, but fill me in. Okay?"

He nodded, looking a little frightened.

She liked him. He was a little green, but he'd come along all right. Writing was his demon, and he was good. Maybe a little more passion in his stories than she liked, but she'd take several more like him.

"Right," he said. "Don't I always?"

She gave a trace of a smile.

"Maybe some friend of his just bought

a new mansion and he wants me to do a house and garden tour," he said over his shoulder, heading down the hallway.

"He wouldn't be asking for you, then," she called after him, then under her breath, "unless he's slipped over the edge. He's certainly been heading that way lately."

Despite the fact Connell was never there, he'd insisted on having an office. And despite the overcrowding outside, Connell's office remained off limits to anyone else unless summoned.

"It's time we did something serious here, don't you think," Connell demanded of English. It was a statement, not a question.

English remained standing, and Connell showed no interest in making the young reporter more comfortable.

"There's a rumor about a new publication. Could stir things up in our quiet little town." Connell was intimidating. He always looked angry and he had a reputation for getting even, which is why, many believed, he got into publishing in the first place.

"You want me to find out . . . ?"

"No, no, no, sit down, sit down. How old are you, English?"

"Twenty-three."

"Ah. Yes. Twenty-three. I'm fifty-five. Did you know that?"

"No, I didn't." Tom English stared at Connell's tie. Fifty bucks at least. The watch? A couple of thou. Paul, the art director, who had met Connell a couple of times, said Connell had gotten a hair job and was obviously going through the change of life, said we'd soon see unbuttoned shirts, sunglasses, and an abundance of jewelry. Paul said he was watching to see when Connell traded his elegant Mercedes sedan for a little convertible sports model. A Porsche, probably.

"Well, I am. And it's time I made a difference. It's time we did something serious here. A city pub can be much more than a home-and-garden magazine. Sarah's a fine editor and all that. But it's time for a little tougher stance. You know what I mean?"

"Well . . . I . . . uh . . ." The story on Connell was that he was as tough as he acted. Marine Corps. Two Purple Hearts. As a reporter, English knew you weren't supposed to be in awe of anybody, yet Connell made him feel uneasy. Very uneasy.

"Street gangs." Connell paused for a moment, letting the words sink in. He stared at Tom English. Tom looked away. When he looked back, Connell's eye twitched. His jaw muscles pulsed. "Nobody's touched the subject. Not our sacred dailies. Not our minicammed, eyewitnessed, electronic brethren. No one. Not really. Not tough, not in-depth. Are you following me?"

"You want me to do a story on street gangs?" Tom English couldn't disguise his joy. "Really, for the magazine?"

"A couple of days ago two young punks murdered some guy on the Eastside." Connell put special emphasis on "murdered." He stood up, walked around his desk, then sat on the edge. "People want to believe these things happen in L.A., New York, not a little sleepy-eyed city like Indianapolis. Things have changed, English. One point two million population, and we now have our share of punks, prostitutes, perverts. I want you to . . . to do the story." Connell looked directly at the young reporter. "You up to it?"

"Yes . . . I think . . ."

"We'll do a feature on gangs," Connell continued, not interested in English's answer. "But I want you to make these punks the central focus. Find out what kind of scum they are. And I want you to work closely with me on it. It's time I got involved around here."

Sarah Mundy looked as if she'd been hit in the gut. "You know I wanted to do the story of that fifteen-year-old girl on death row. I send him the usual story list and he faxes back his usual dictum. No, advertisers don't want depressing news, he says. I wanted to do an in-depth feature on that black kid who died in the backseat of a police car. Advertisers don't pay for controversy, he says. The hottest topic we've been able to cover is the pros and cons of cosmetic surgery."

"It's a good story, Sarah. I want to do it. How do you want me to handle this?"

"I don't know why the fuck he's paying an editor." Sarah Mundy stood up, walked straight out the door leading to the parking lot. She was gone long enough to count to a hundred, and came in looking calm but determined. "Do it, Tom. Do a good job. It's the kind of story I've always wanted to do. I'm just pissed that it's only a good story when it's his idea. I'll help you any way I can."

"He wants it in the next issue," English said, waiting for the big blow.

"Does he, now? Well then, he shall have it. You have two days."

"Sarah?"

She was only half listening. Finally, she turned toward him. "Yeah?"

"He wants a big story, a really big story. . . ." English was plaintive.

"Tell the . . . tell him we'll make it a two-part series. Three, maybe. Tell him we'll publish a goddam book for him."

While she was outside, Sarah Mundy screamed. She screamed very loud, so loud, in fact, she stopped traffic and a gentleman brought his silver Honda to the sidewalk, got out, and asked if she was all right.

"Yes, I'm fine now," she told the young man. He wasn't badlooking. Brown curly hair. Tall, lean. He wore a gray suit, blue shirt, and red paisley tie. The car was a deluxe model Honda, an Accord with a sun roof and all the bells and whistles.

He smiled at her.

"I was just letting off steam, releasing the stress. I'm sorry, I didn't mean to scare anybody." She smiled in return, wondering if he found her attractive. No golden ring around his finger. She checked that right off. Nothing of that kind escaped her notice.

"Not a bad idea," he said, still standing there, still looking at her. "I've always thought Americans needed a wailing wall. Only not just for deaths, for screaming your head off."

Sarah Mundy laughed. It wasn't altogether sincere. She found it amusing, but she found it more important to let him know she liked him. She brushed back her hair.

"My name is Sarah Mundy," she said, extending her hand. She was used to acting like a man. A newspaperwoman couldn't do otherwise.

He took it, shook it surprisingly firmly. "Daniel Sutton." He smiled again. He was awfully young, she thought. "I have to go," he said, "I'm late."

"Stop in for coffee," she said almost too quickly. "Sometime. Anytime except the last ten days of the month. I work at *Metro Monthly.*" She gave the hitchhiking thumb over her shoulder in the general direction of the modest building.

"Sure," he said, running toward his car.

She should have told him she was the editor and not the girl answering the telephones, she thought. She saw her reflection in the office window, and what she noticed first was her gray hair, her slightly out-of-date glasses, not to mention her wardrobe. And especially the fact that without makeup she looked older than her forty-three years.

She would have to do something about that. Sarah Mundy also would have to do something about James A. Connell, the man with whom she'd had a year-long affair some fifteen years ago. He'd bought her the magazine, at least that was what he'd said. Funny or maybe not so funny, she had only flimsy proof of that. Her name was nowhere on the papers.

That afternoon, Sarah Mundy decided to make some changes. She would dump her little two-bedroom home near Glendale Shopping Center. She would get her hair done, get some decent clothes and she would take over the magazine.

It wouldn't be difficult. If he wouldn't honor his words, she knew some things about him. Some he knew she knew, others he did not. One way or the other, she would own the magazine. She would be comfortable, pretty, highly eligible and no handsome young man would miss the opportunity to have a cup of coffee with her.

"Daniel Sutton," she said aloud as she walked back through the door. "Danny, there's a little restaurant I know called Something Different, would you meet me there at eight tonight?" That's what she'd say to this young man when he stopped by and saw the new Sarah Mundy.

She laughed. "James A. Connell, you are going to learn or burn."

FOUR

"I need more than that," Shanahan said into the telephone.

"That's all I can give you," Rafferty said. "I shouldn't even be talking with you. I'm at a goddam pay phone at a 7-Eleven. Let me explain something to you, since you're apparently not too quick on picking up the subtleties."

"Please do. I can always stand a lesson in personal behavior from such an exemplary police officer."

"Look, nobody knows this yet, but they

soon will. The corpse is a cop. Undercover. A cop was killed. And as far as the department is concerned, those two little bastards are cop killers. Do you know what that means? That means that if they find out I hired a private shlep to clear them, I'm not only persona non gratis, I'm probably persona non existis. Comprende? Get the info from Edie."

"I can't get the police report from your little factory girl."

"The cop was undercover. Coke. Don't know much more than that."

"Who was he working on?"

"I can't tell you."

"It's all an act, isn't it, Rafferty? All you want me to do is ask Edie a couple of questions, so you can look like you care. You hire me 'cause I'm cheap and you know I don't have any police connections except you."

"I tell you, I don't know. You never give me a break, do you?"

"You can't tell me what he was working on?"

"Undercover. You know what that means? Look, Shanahan. Puckett was a good guy—"

"Yeah sure, you were a bosom buddy."

"No, I'm not saying that. He moved in different circles."

"What kind of circles, Rafferty?"

"You know there are all kinds of cops out there in society, just like there's all kinds of rent-a-cops. There's the scuzzbags, then there's the marginal cops. You know, like me. A little lazy, playing the margins, cutting a few corners, getting angry and acting like a normal human being under stress. Puckett was one of those cops they used to picture on magazine covers, offering a kid an ice cream cone. The only thing negative, if you call it negative was he liked women a whole lot. On the other hand, he was tough as nails. Fair and tough. A real pro. Public service. Smart and honest. If Puckett wasn't black, he'd've been chief of police."

"Okay, okay. He was a paradigm of virtue. But maybe, just maybe, he was killed in the line of duty and not by a couple of amateur burglars?"

"All right, if I find out anything, I'll try to get it to her. But don't you realize that my seeing her before this thing is cleared up is not too smart either. You don't know what this mess is going to do with my love life."

"You're a sweetheart, Rafferty. You think they did it?"

"Who?"

"Did the little bastards kill the cop?"

"How the hell should I know? Doesn't look good. Edie's brother's fingerprints were found on the wallet. The other kid's prints were on the windowsill. We have a witness who saw them around the house at the time of death. Then, if that weren't enough, they passed one of the bills—marked bills, for Christ sake, because it was drug money—at the neighborhood liquor store. The owner will testify to that."

"So what am I doing? Even if they didn't do it, they're gonna pay for it."

"I told Edie I'd help her. Couple of days and nothing shows up, you go bye-bye."

"I see," Shanahan said. "Okay, Rafferty, stay away from the doughnuts and the monster Pepsi's." He slammed the phone down, hoping it would break Rafferty's eardrums.

"Morning glory," Dierdorf said, sipping coffee out of a stained mug. He stood up, showing the wrinkles in his size 48 polyester suit. "I got some news for you." He ran the palms of his hands back across his oily, silver-haired temples.

"So what you in such a good mood for, Dorf?" Marty said. Marty was a little smaller than his brother-in-law. He too had silver hair, what there was of it. Mere wisps over the ears. Marty Ray owned the club. Dierdorf managed it for him. "You get some last night you didn't have to pay for?"

"C'mon, c'mon, you know I would do nothing like that, 'cause of Phyllis and Helen. Huh? You know that. Hey! Marty? Right?"

"I don't know that. You have last night's totals? How much at the door?"

"Twenty-five hundred."

"What about the bar?"

"Eight hundred," Dierdorf replied.

"Shit. Might as well not serve liquor, for Chrissakes. Everybody's lookin' at the flesh. Nobody's drinkin'."

"It's in the papers, Marty."

"What's in the papers? Prohibition? Nobody's drinkin' anymore? What the hell are you talkin' about?"

"Shepard went to meet his maker," Dierdorf said, smiling. "Only he wasn't

Shepard. Some cop by the name of Puckett."

"What? You pregnant? What you grinning about?"

"You wanted him out of the way."

"Yeah, so now he is."

Dierdorf was still smiling.

"Would you wipe that stupid smile off your goofy face," Marty said.

"Hey, Marty. You happy about this, or what?"

"I'm happy. So, now figure out a way to get the bar bill up, okay? What in the hell are you still smiling for?" Marty headed for his back office.

"What would you say if I told you I took care of the matter for you."

Marty stopped, then started back up the steps. "What matter?" Suddenly it hit him. He stopped, frozen. What was Dierdorf telling him? That he had killed the cop? "You kidding? You can't step on a roach, afraid it's a relative. Listen, tell the girls I want a longer break between shows. If the crowd gets a little bored, they'll drink a little more."

"Or go somewhere else," Dierdorf mumbled. "Marty?"

"What?"

"What about Shepard, I mean—"

"Don't know any Shepard. Don't know any Puckett, and neither do you."

Marty sat at his desk, shoved aside piles of paper, found his glasses. He pulled a handkerchief out of his pocket, wiped the lenses, then his forehead.

"Who does he think he's kidding?" Marty mumbled. He picked up the phone and punched 1, then area code 313, then a seven-digit number. "My luck," he said into the mouthpiece. "My sister picks a real winner. When his deck got shuffled, a few of the cards fell out . . . Hello . . . this is Marty Ray. I need to talk to . . ."

"So, you ain't talking to me, Billy?" Leo asked. His right knee went up and down like a jackhammer as they sat waiting in the small room.

"Don't use 'ain't.' " Billy said.

"I don't need any English lesson, Billy. You're pissed. So get it out so we can get back to normal."

Billy's laugh was unexpected, but it turned into a snarl at the end.

"Jesus fucking Christ, Leo. I'm not pissed over some little stupid trick of yours. Because you couldn't wait to spend the fuckin' money, we're going to spend the rest of our lives in a meat locker. Or maybe we're going sit in the 'lectric chair and get our buns roasted. We're not going to get back to normal, understand?"

The door opened. A tall, thin, black woman with high cheekbones and serious glasses entered. She carried a briefcase.

"My name is Bailey," she said approaching the table.

"So?" Leo said.

"So I am your attorney."

Leo rolled his eyes. "You? Who says?"

"The court says." She sat down, unlocked the briefcase with a tiny key and pulled out a yellow legal pad and a pen. "Which one are you?" she asked, making eye contact with Leo.

"Leo Porter," he said sullenly.

"Then you must be William Chatwin?"

Billy looked up, then up toward the light coming through the small window. Leo laughed.

"Ain't nobody calls him William," Leo said.

"Well, I do, Leonard."

FIVE

For Shanahan it was the kind of clear October morning he remembered from his childhood. Things weren't particularly rosy, though. Then again, they weren't all that rosy when he was a kid. On the drive over to see the lady with the wayward husband, he kept thinking about Maureen, about the phone calls, how strange and unfamiliar she seemed.

He had thought about the age question before. Actually, Shanahan thought it was impossible from the beginning. A forty-five-year-old woman and a man approaching seventy? It was Maureen who convinced him it wasn't a problem. And finally, he had felt secure. Now, that gnawing, stomach-churning doubt came back. She was going to take off. Shanahan was almost sure of it. Maureen could do that. Pack her bags and be out in a split second.

Looking up at the clear blue sky, he wondered if he could simply just put her out of his mind. Altogether. Pretend she had been a dream, pretend that it all had been a pleasant dream. He looked up and realized he'd missed his turn. He turned on Thirty-eighth Street, passed the Broadmoor Country Club, turned into the Museum of Art and around in the parking lot, then headed back to the street leading into Golden Hills.

"Good morning, Mrs. Dunfy," Shanahan said to the rather severe woman who was checking up on her husband.

"Mr. Shanahan, you needn't have driven over, but I do appreciate the personal touch."

There was a sarcastic edge to the tone of her voice as it echoed off the walls of the entry hall. She led him to a sitting room, all yellow and sunny, chairs and sofas upholstered in soft floral prints.

"I take it this means you've discovered something. I want you to know that you don't have to be delicate, Mr. Shanahan. I've suspected Warren's dual nature for a long time. Though I don't approve of homosexuality, I'd like to know so that I may help him."

"Yes," he said, standing despite her gesture to sit. "Mrs. Dunfy, does Mr. Dunfy have a daughter, perhaps by an earlier marriage, or do the two of you have a niece maybe? Living in an apartment complex on Westfield Boulevard?"

"Why no." Her face broke a bit, as did her voice. She was clearly surprised. She sat down. "Are you telling me that Warren has been having a sexual liaison with a child? A little girl?"

"Mrs. Dunfy, I have no idea what kind of relationship Mr. Dunfy has with this woman, and I assure you she is a woman, not a child. It could be something other than sexual," Shanahan said, thinking he'd just given Mr. Dunfy a benefit of the doubt so wide it could have encompassed Dallas.

"You don't know? Isn't it your job to know? What about photographs?"

"Mrs. Dunfy, I was hired to find out what your hushand was doing when he wasn't at the office or at home. I have. I don't peek through keyholes. I don't take photos of people in compromising positions."

"That bastard!" she exclaimed, and left the room. "I'll kill him."

Next stop: Edie Porter.

"I hope you don't mind if I eat while we're talkin'," Edie Porter said, taking a sandwich—honeyloaf and mayonnaise on white bread—from a clear poly sack. "I only got thirty minutes.

She leaned back against the concrete block wall next to the employee entrance to Upshank Manufacturing. Shanahan had trouble imagining Rafferty and this girl together.

"What do you know about all this?"

"I don't know much. Just that they got Leo. It's not that he's never been in trouble or nothin'. He has. Plenty. But not like this. And I know everybody always says this about people they love, but I know Leo and I know he'd never kill nobody."

"What about Billy? You know Billy too, don't you?"

"Well yeah. He practically grew up with us. And he's strange. Quiet so you don't know what he's thinking and all, and that hair down over his eyes so nobody can see him. But I can't believe Billy would either. I mean do that. Kill somebody." She took a bite of her sandwich and seemed to be considering something else. "Not unless he changed an awful lot since he moved up here." She caught a dribble of mayonnaise with her finger and put it to her lips.

"Where do they live?"

"I don't know. I know I should, but Leo never said. I got the feeling they were just hanging out."

"What about parents, Miss Porter?"

"I'm afraid they're not gonna account for much in this." She said it with a look that said she didn't want to get into it. It wasn't hard to guess why either. Some nests you can't wait to get out of. Sometimes you even get a premature nudge.

"And Billy's parents?"

"About the same, as far as I know," she said, taking a bite out of her sandwich and washing it down with Diet Coke.

"What about any other friends? Who else did they hang around with?"

"I'm sorry. I'm not much help. They never really hung out with other people. They were together, just the two of them."

"Girlfriends maybe?"

"Ohhh!" she said, looking like she'd just remembered where she put a winning lottery ticket. "There was a girl Leo talked about. Lisa! That's it, Lisa."

"Lisa who?"

Now Edie Porter looked grief-stricken. "He never said."

"Christ, Shanahan, how in the hell you find

me here?" Rafferty scooted away from the table, a disgusted look on his face.

"I'm a detective. You like cheesecake. They serve cheesecake here. Deduction. Detective work. They ever teach you things like that there in the department?"

"No, they teach us about how P.I.'s are all dickheads."

"What the hell is that?" Shanahan asked, pointing to the only plate on the table with food still on it.

"Swiss Bavarian chocolate almond and praline cheesecake. Tell you a secret, though. It's too rich."

Shanahan pulled out a chair and sat down. "Really?"

"Oh, now you want to be sociable. You throw me out of your house after refusing to feed me. You hang up in my ear so hard my teeth shook, and now you want to have a little tête-à-tête. I'm flattered."

"I called. Nobody's talking, and they're not letting anybody in to see these two dangerous criminals except people who have parental or legal papers."

"So?"

"So, Mr. Police Lieutenant. I hear you're pretty good at pulling strings, and I need a few strings pulled so I can talk with them."

"Ooooh no. I told you already. I don't even like the idea of being seen with you. We agreed. Talk with Edie." He began making patterns on the top of the cheesecake with his fork.

"I talked with Edie. She's a nice girl. But she should be turning letters on a game show. All I have now is the first name of some girlfriend of Leo's. Lisa somebody. No last name. I have to talk with the kids."

"Listen to me a minute. You know the beloved prosecutor? Mr. Robert Silvers? First thing out of his mouth this morning? 'We're going for the death penalty.' Now you know what that did? That got the media types buzzing. What we have here is the theme line for his political campaign for mayor. The 'I'm tough on crime' issue. Then our little chapter of the Civil Liberties Union says the kids aren't adults. Silvers says the Indiana Civil Liberties Union is full of commies and perverts and that under the law he can fry their butts if he wants to."

"I appreciate your commentary on local politics, which I'm sure you're very knowledgeable of and very good at, but I don't care."

"Oh, but you will. You know, about eleven this morning, there were five TV camera crews, at least three reporters from each daily, and get this—even a reporter from *Metro Monthly* magazine, for Chrissake. Even the fluffs want in on this one. And I don't think they want Billy and Leo's choice of best restaurant. I mean I half expected to find Dan Rather standing outside the Marion County Jail.

"So?"

"So, my thick-headed P.I., I hope you don't mind being in the limelight, because anyone connected with this case is going to be either a darling or a devil to the press. They are going to be investigating everybody, including the investigators."

Shanahan sat back in his chair, sighing.

"I'm sorry, Shanahan. I really can't afford being seen with you. And the longer this thing goes on, the more dangerous it is for me. Look, there's a woman. Her last name is Bailey. She's been appointed defense counsel. Actually, she volunteered for the job. Talk to her. Maybe she can help. Chances are she needs you as much as you need her."

"I'm not sure I need any of this hassle," Shanahan said, thinking about the check he was going to get from Mrs. Dunfy. He headed for the door.

"Two days," Rafferty said. "If you don't turn up anything, we both quit worrying about it."

"Two days," Shanahan repeated.

"Shanahan! One more thing. This Bailey woman. She's black."

"So?" Shanahan had stopped, turned, and now took a few steps back toward the table.

"The cop who was killed was black," Rafferty said. "You understand what I'm saying?"

"I rarely understand what you say. Maybe it's because you talk with your mouth full."

"Here's a black woman with a great local rep and a lucrative practice, who volunteered—at little or no remuneration—to defend a couple of white kids accused of killing a black man. Doesn't it seem strange to you?" Shanahan turned toward the door again. "One more thing . . ."

"That's two more things, Rafferty, even Trigger could count to two."

"How'd you know I was here?"

"Cheesecake, Rafferty. I told you. Deduction. You know, you're gonna die with food in your mouth."

SIX

"I need to talk with the kids," Shanahan said to Mrs. Bailey. She hadn't said much so far. She sat behind her desk, a two-inch-thick slab of glass on rectangular marble pedestals. He could look down through the top to see the expensive red marble floor and one of her expensive shoes doing an impatient tap dance upon it.

"Then I think you need to tell me who you work for," she said again, this time curtly. Her eyes were impatient behind the thick glasses.

"I told you. Edie Porter."

"Edie Porter cannot afford a Big Mac, Mr. Shanahan, let alone a private investigator."

"A friend of hers is helping her out."

"Now we're getting somewhere. Who's the friend?"

"I'm not permitted to say."

"That's unfortunate for you, Mr. Shanahan."

"For us, Mrs. Bailey. You seem to forget

that you are supposed to be proving their innocence."

"Wrong on two counts. I'm *Ms.* Bailey. And I am to provide Leonard Porter and William Chatwin the best legal counsel possible, not necessarily prove their innocence."

"So you think they did it? Did they admit they did it, Msssss. Bailey?"

"Mr. Shanahan." She stood up, walked around the edge of the desk to the French doors that led out into the foyer. "I'd prefer to conduct my own investigations, utilizing the services of reputable firms, not a part-time detective working out of his living room. And tell your client, Lieutenant Rafferty, that his trysts with Edie Porter are safe with me. By the way, if you do discover something you think might be useful, please contact my secretary and he'll pass it along to me. Thank you."

"What have you got?" James Connell hovered over Tom English as he in turn hovered over his Macintosh computer in the tiny cubicle.

"Uhhhh . . ." English scanned the pages for inspiration. "Not much. Two kids, picked up a couple of times but let go. The sister, an 'Edie Porter,' was given custody. Nothing violent. Petty theft. No address. Cops believe the kids were caught in the act of robbery and killed the guy."

"Only the guy was a cop, English. And it wasn't a couple of kids, English. Cop killers. What gang? Did you get the name of the gang?"

English could feel Connell's breath on the top of his head, sweeping over his forehead. "Oh . . . yeah . . . un . . . well." English swallowed with difficulty. "Anyway, no gang. Not as far as I could tell."

"Look, English." Connell sat down on the reporter's desk. "This is our story. We're gonna do something here. I want you to get the mug shots, all right? We'll put the grainy photos, numbers and all, on the cover in black and white with a graphic of a bloody bayonet. Fantastic. Then I want you to interview the sister, the ICLU, the prosecutor. Check out the neighborhood. And I'll get you in to see the little bastards."

English was about to tell him that he'd already done everything but interview the kids. He'd talked to the people in the neighborhood; Mr. Price, the liquor store owner; the prosecutor; the guy at the Civil Liberties Union. But Connell had a funny look on his face.

"Yeah." Connell was quiet for a very long time. It seemed like a cloud passed over his eyes. "Just listen." He stood up slowly, looked over the row of cubicles. "We have to establish the dynamics, so you know what to ask and what to take down. You know what I mean? The dynamics of the story. A cop—a black cop, no less—is killed in the line of duty. The prosecutor doing his best to get the punk scum off the streets while the bleeding heart liberals at the ICLU will try to get them off." He was still talking but it seemed like a real effort.

"The ICLU has protested, but they're not sure they have an interest in the case right now," English said.

"Oh, they will. That's what they do best, get murderers and thieves outta jail."

"What if it's not that way? I mean maybe they didn't do it?"

"C'mon, c'mon, c'mon. They got the fingerprints, they passed the money. They were there. This isn't the movies, son. And another thing, I don't want you talking about how rough they had it. All right? Nobody in this town wants to read a story about troubled youth. That kind of shit doesn't cut it anymore.

Paul Berensen's curly red hair popped up over the padded cubicle wall. "Mr. Connell, there's someone on the phone. Wouldn't say who."

"I've got to go," Connell said abruptly. He hurried back into his office.

"Weird shit," Paul said. "Wish he'd go back to his various boardrooms and leave us poor chill'un alone."

"Did you get the stats, Paul?" It was Sarah Mundy's voice.

"They sent Xeroxes," Paul said. "Just one more classy advertiser." Paul's head disappeared, but they could hear him singing, "Hey big spender, spend a little time with me."

"Cute," Sarah said. "How's it going?" She took her publisher's spot in the cubicle.

"I don't know, Sarah. I thought I was going to like doing this story."

"What's the matter?"

"Mr. Connell seems to have written it before we've even gathered the facts."

"Oh, that," she said, as if that were the most common practice in the world. She left English, who now stared blankly at the words on the screen:

Nobody seems to know much about Leo Porter and William Chatwin. They don't much care either. But everyone seems to believe one of them stabbed a policeman while the other watched. It was all that simple. They were nabbed and the investigation closed twenty-four hours after the crime was committed.

English ran the cursor over the paragraph, highlighting it in black. Then he erased it. "Shit," he said.

Shanahan still smarted from the attorney's remarks. There was nothing he could do. She knew about him. He knew nothing of her. He felt as if she'd cut out his heart with an ice pick. He drove down Washington Street to the house where the undercover cop, Sam Puckett, was iced for real.

The front door was sealed and banded. So was the back. "What the hell," he muttered as he approached a side window. He took out his penknife and cut the tape and forced open the window. The smell was familiar—that sickening sweet smell of death— reminding him of other times, other places he'd longed to forget.

Brown splotches of dried blood were everywhere. The ceiling, the walls, floors, over the worn-out furniture. It would have appeared to be a mad bludgeoning or a massacre. How could so much come from the body of one human being? Shanahan knew the answer. Something had struck the heart.

Nothing else around. Empty fast-food bags, wadded-up waxed paper wrappers from a doughnut shop, coffee-stained paper cups. A deck of cards. It was a typical stakeout house, or in this case, a contact house. No trace of ownership. No personal artifacts. Shanahan wasn't surprised he found nothing to help create a portrait of the victim. Did he need one? The man was killed either because he was in the wrong place at the wrong time or because he was a cop. There was a third possibility. Something personal. Deeply personal.

He called Rafferty from the phone booth in front of a discount gas station on Washington Street. "I need an address, Rafferty. Samuel Puckett."

"For Chrissake, what do you need that for?"

"I need it. Get it."

"It's on Meridian, below Thirty-eighth.

I know. Southeast corner of Thirty-sixth. Apartment building. Name should be on the door."

"I know the one. A postage-stamp swimming pool in front?"

"Yeah, I think so. He never invited me over to go swimming."

"What did he invite you over for?"

"Nothing, Shanahan. I sold him a stereo and took it over to him. What in the hell am I explaining myself to you for?"

"Beats me. Anything else I should know?"

"Like what?"

"The obvious," Shanahan said. "What was he working on?"

"Don't know."

"Come on!"

"Look, like I said, he had a line on some cocaine dealing, but as far as I can tell, even he didn't know the connection. Last report was that he thought it had something to do with either the massage parlors or, more than likely, one of the nudie clubs."

"Which one?"

"Don't know. Nobody knows. He thought there could be somebody inside the force connected in some way. But don't get hot to trot on the corrupt cop angle, he just wasn't sure, that's all. So he played it real close to the vest."

"Somebody got pretty close to his vest. Did they find prints on the weapon?"

"None."

"Stabbed in the heart?"

"Yeah. Real messy, they tell me."

"What kind of blade was it?"

"What do you mean? What difference does it make?"

"C'mon, Rafferty. A hunting knife? A butcher knife? A Swiss army knife?

"You think maybe a Cub Scout did it?" Rafferty laughed.

"Well, that's about what they're saying, isn't it?"

"Get off me, Shanahan. Okay? I hope you get them cleared for Edie's sake, but they aren't the Cleaver kids." Rafferty laughed. "Maybe they are the Cleaver kids. Why don't you check with your buddies at the coroner's office?"

"I don't have a buddy at the coroner's office."

"Don't you watch TV and the movies? All you guys got friends down there."

"Okay. I'll tell 'em you told me to call."

"Bayonet. I heard that. I didn't see the report. I don't know for sure. You satisfied?" There was no laughter in Rafferty's voice.

"No. What kind of bayonet?"

"What the hell difference does it make? You're getting on my nerves, Shanahan."

"Could make a difference. Japanese? American? German? Italian?"

"You think the Japs did it? Get outta here. And I mean it, Shanahan, don't call me here!"

"Don't worry, Rafferty, I told 'em I was your mother."

While he was in the neighborhood, Shanahan stopped by the liquor store where Leo passed the marked hundred-dollar bill. He bought a bottle of J.W. Dant and quizzed the owner, one Mr. Price. Price was balding. What hair he had was carrot red, and matted down like a used Brillo pad. Price remembered the kids. Billy hung back; Leo did the negotiating. Apparently Price didn't mind selling booze to minors, but got a little nervous when he read the papers.

"I wondered where them kids got a hundred bucks. Usually they come in here with scrunched-up singles and a bunch of change."

Price remembered what they bought, what time they bought it and what they were wearing. "Hell, they always wear the same thing. Kids ain't got no other clothes. Both of 'em wear them jean jackets. The loud one had on a black tee-shirt, something 'bout Megadeth on it, and other one, the one that hung back, he was wearin' a red and black plaid shirt. Got it on film," Price said, looking up at the little video camera above the cash register with a red, blinking light.

"That right?" Shanahan said.

"Yep."

"You mean you actually have tape in that thing?"

"Yep. Sure do. Keep it for thirty days just in case somebody robs me and busts out the camera. I got his picture anyway 'cause he probably cased the place first. You get robbed as many times as I have, you get pretty cagey."

"When I first saw you, I told myself now there's a pretty cagey guy. You still have it, then?"

"You mean the one with the boys on it?"

"That's the one. Be willing to buy it from you."

Shanahan sat in the back room, scooting

aside back issues of *Hustler* and *Monsieur* and *Escapade*, going over the videos. The place smelled like a toilet. The grainy black and white video fluttered, tenuous, ghost-like images in oxide. Shanahan was reminded how tawdry lives could be, how easily the world could be reduced to one long despairing gasp.

There they were. Leo, bold and confrontational. Billy, observing, half hidden by the lock of dark hair over his eyes. Price was extracting an extra commission for selling the booze. Leo got eighty dollars back. Twenty bucks for a six-pack of Bartles & Jaymes.

"You're one cagey guy, Mr. Price," Shanahan told him. "Tell me one more thing.

"You saw the kids the night of the murder, right?"

"I did. I told the police that. Just a couple of minutes before they figure the cop bought it."

"So what were they wearing?"

"Told you. Same shit. I never seen the one kid without that Megadeth tee-shirt. Far as I know, they never change clothes."

Shanahan drove to Upshank. It was quarter

till three in the afternoon, but it could have been any time. The gray sky held no clue. It could have been after the Holocaust. His stomach growled and he realized that part of his depression came from not eating. He was tempted to open the bottle of bourbon, but he had things to do.

The factory wasn't particularly uplifting either. Shanahan walked through the rows of clunking machines until he found Edie Porter.

"Fifteen minutes," she said. "I can't leave till three. I've been written up three times already. They'd fire me."

Shanahan went to the lunchroom, put sixty cents in the vending machine and retrieved a "cherry-flavored" pie.

SEVEN

Sarah Mundy stuck her head in Tom English's cube.

"You're on your own now, kid."

"What?"

"I did it. I'm not sure if I quit or was fired, but I'm now a part of *Metro Monthly*'s rich and proud history."

"Sarah! You can't do that."

"Done. And frankly, I feel marvelous. No more house and garden stories. No more First Lady stories. And no more, pardon my use of jargon, fucking First Lady of Indiana stories. No more recipes. No more contrived best french fries in the city stories."

"What are you going to do? My God, what am I going to do?" English said.

She leaned down, kissed him on the cheek. "You're going to do fine. If I find work, I'll send for you. On this murder thing, if you have to, write a story for him and write the real one for yourself. Even if it never gets published."

"Who's going to be editor? Mr. Connell doesn't know how."

"That's his problem," she said with a smile. "I'm sorry. It'll work out. Tell you a secret. I'll probably be back."

Edie had rehearsed it. "My name is Edie Porter, Leo Porter's sister, and this is Mr. Chatwin, Billy's dad." It would all be so easy—Shanahan passing as Billy's dad. And that was about the only way Shanahan was going to get to talk with the boys.

What Shanahan hadn't counted on was

finding Ms. Bailey, her ebony face smooth and frozen like an African carving, sitting there with Leo and Billy. Only her eyes, magnified by the thick lens of her glasses, moved when he came in the room.

Shanahan stared at her, then the guard, as Edie finished her memorized intro. ". . . and this is Mr. Chatwin, Billy's . . ."

"What the fuck . . ." Leo interjected.

". . . dad," Edie said, her voice getting very weak.

Bailey stood up. Shanahan slumped back against the wall, wondering if he was about to get an adjoining cell.

"Billy," she said calmly, "say hello to your father. He's obviously gone to a lot of trouble to see you."

"What the . . ." Leo continued.

"Hi, pops," Billy said a little too loudly, to override Leo's protestations, then noncomittally, "How're they hanging?"

Leo giggled, settled back in his chair.

"Thank you," Bailey said to the guard, who got the same cold, certain dismissal Shanahan had received earlier in the day.

"Sit down Mr. Shan—er, Mr. Chatwin. The problem is," Bailey adjusted her glasses, folded her hands neatly on the tabletop as if she were about to give a lecture to high school students, "the prosecution will make no deals. Murder during the commission of a felony."

Billy pretended to slit his own throat. "Death," he said almost gleefully.

Edie wept. Bailey ignored her.

"I'm afraid that in the State of Indiana, the death penalty applies to sixteen-year-olds," Bailey said coolly. "Two witnesses will testify they saw Leonard and William on the lawn of . . . the policeman's, for the lack of a better word, residence a few days prior to the death, and most certainly again on the day and time of his death. Both sets of fingerprints taken from the scene match those of our young defendants here. The money they passed—and had on them—was marked, recorded, and given to the victim prior to his death."

She spoke quickly and matter of factly, all the while looking directly at Shanahan. It was a professional briefing. No extraneous information, no personal comments on the facts, and, clearly, no emotion.

"There is also a new piece of evidence which indicates the blood found on the soles of Leonard's shoes matches that of the victim. Now, as I said, there will be no plea bargaining. If they choose to make a guilty plea, it is possible the judge will take that into account."

"We didn't do it," Leo said. He walked over to his sister, putting his arm on her shoulder. "Honest, Edie."

"As you can see . . . I'm not quite sure how to proceed, except that we have an overwhelming wall of circumstantial evidence to surmount. Therefore, I am willing to accept help from any quarter."

"Oh, thank you," Shanahan said, dryly. Then to Leo, "I want to know how you could be so stupid as to burgle a house while the guy was still in it."

"Who are you anyways?" Leo asked.

"He's a private detective employed by your sister," Jennifer Bailey said, glancing back at Shanahan. "So answer the question."

"You're a detective? Gimme a break."

"Answer the question," Bailey said firmly.

"He wasn't in it," Leo said hostilely.

"He was and he wasn't," Billy said, without any emotion.

"We saw him leave. Only when we got inside, there he was stuck pretty good. Blood all over. We ain't stupid. Hell, that's why we chose the fuckin' place." He looked at his sister. "Sorry, Edie. We decided to do that house 'cause there was only one guy livin' there." Leo was pissed.

"You were too stupid to report it to the police." Shanahan said.

"Yeah, like we'd'a been here a fuckin' day earlier. Like we coulda said to the cops, 'Yeah, well, we were like breakin' into this place and happened to find this dead guy.' Like that?"

"Okay, guys. I want to know everything from the day you first started watching Puckett's house until they booked you into these fine accommodations. I want to know what you wore, what you ate, where you ate it, what you thought, what you said, who you talked to, when you sneezed and how many times."

"We don't have to take this shit from you," Leo said. "Right, Billy?"

"Right, Leo. What do we care?" Billy tossed his head back in another futile attempt to keep the hair out of his eyes. "I mean these guys in jail are real cute. Then if we're lucky, we get us the chance to have our buns punched, then afterward they get roasted like they do over at the Burger King. *Zzzzzzt.*" Billy went into fake muscle spasms.

"I got this girl, Lisa," Leo said without further encouragement, "and she told us about this house and how this guy leaves every day at the same time and . . ."

"I think we're in a world of hurt," Leo said as the guard led the two kids down the long hallway. "I mean we got Grandpa and the cleaning lady on our side. You ever see a private detective that old? He ain't no Magnum." He waved the card Shanahan had given them in the event they thought of something else.

Billy snatched the card, didn't say anything. His eyes were busy checking out windows and doors as he went. Once inside, Billy called Leo over and whispered.

"Somebody tries something funny, tell 'em you got the drips."

"What are you talking about?"

"Tell 'em you got a disease or something."

Einstein was ready to eat. There was no mistaking it. He sat on Shanahan's desk, next to the blinking answering machine, creating his usual cacophony of groans, whines, and howls. Shanahan was late and Einstein was hungry.

Casey was on the line of scrimmage,

which was the doorway to the kitchen. To get his food, Einstein would have to fake the dog to the left or right or, as he had done on occasion, go through his legs. Einstein knew better than to try to jump. Casey was great with anything in the air. This time there was a standoff. Einstein stood in front of Casey as Shanahan opened up a can of Nine Lives liver and bacon dinner.

Casey became impatient, lunged forward. Einstein zipped around, a gray streak on the linoleum. Casey turned, on Einstein's tail, which was now airborne. Einstein maneuvered a crash landing on the kitchen counter, scattering the unwashed coffee cups and bourbon glasses. Who said all cats are graceful?

After all these few years, it never dawned on Shanahan he could avoid the daily confrontation by feeding Casey first until just now. "The obvious, isn't it?" he said to Einstein, who was devouring his food as if he hadn't eaten in weeks. "Take it easy, kid." He put some vermicelli in a pan of boiling water and set it back on one of the only two electric burners that worked. In five minutes he would have his dinner—a plate of pasta in lemon, butter, and garlic sauce.

Shanahan let Casey out and watched as

the oddly spotted and splotched dog went galumphing off through the mud. When you gotta go, you gotta go, mud or no mud. Shanahan went to the answering machine. "Beep." The first message was from Mrs. Dunfy, who offered Shanahan a thousand dollars to get photos of Mr. Dunfy's young mistress. Not a compromising photo, just a photo and a name. She also implied Shanahan wouldn't get paid anything if he refused. "Beep."

The second voice belonged to Maureen. It was cool and distant, as if she were making an appointment with her dentist. "I'll be up tomorrow night to pick up some clothes. Dad is worse. My sister is here now, but I'll need to take care of things here. No need to call."

He felt the stab in the pit of his stomach. Then it felt like his stomach had simply disappeared. They were familiar feelings, ones he had early in their relationship, when he believed she had left him. He couldn't let that happen, or at least, not the feeling. He thought that at his age, he would be beyond this kind of puppy-love emotion.

Shanahan went to the screen door, let Casey in. Saw the muddy tracks on the hardwood floor, noticed how the mud

Casey had tromped through had splashed up on him and splotched Casey's already strangely colored coat.

"It's just too obvious, isn't it?" The splotches on Casey's fur and Maureen returning to pick up her clothes connected in Shanahan's mind. He was sure Leo and Billy didn't do it. It wasn't possible. The blood would have splattered on them, on their clothing. And the guy that owned the liquor store, Price, said the kids were wearing the same clothes before and after, more or less. No way around that unless they came dressed in yellow slickers. Now, if they didn't do it, who did?

Shanahan was pretty sure his theory about the clothing wouldn't be enough to get them off. So he had to find out more about Leo and Billy's statement that they saw someone they presumed was Puckett walking down to the Taco Bell.

The obvious answer was the subject of Puckett's investigation. He'd come too close, been discovered. Were there any other possibilities? There were three other possibilities. One, that somebody besides Leo and Billy tried to rob him. Doubtful. Two, could be personal. Bad debt, some sort of family argument, jealous husband

. . . or jilted lover. Three, could be somebody who found out Puckett was a narc. Somebody or somebodies who were about to lose major bucks or maybe didn't want to go to jail.

Shanahan decided to check out Puckett's living quarters. He went into the bedroom to get a jacket, saw the unmade bed.

"Oh Maureen, why do you do this to me?" As always, he embarrassed himself with his self-pity. He looked at Casey. "Hey, I didn't have anybody till she came along, did I? I got along all right, didn't I? Stay off the sofa while I'm gone."

Before Shanahan shut the door behind him, the dog climbed up on the sofa. A good listener, he thought, but he does as he damn well pleases.

He was half tempted to drive down to see Maureen; maybe that's what she wanted, but was too proud to ask. She was as independent as they came, and wouldn't like the idea of someone thinking she couldn't handle this by herself. Shanahan turned instead to go to Puckett's apartment on Meridian Street. He was glad to have an alternative. He was glad he had gotten Puckett's address from Rafferty. He had planned to do a little personal reconnaissance. Now was a better time than most to pass a few late evening hours.

It was after eleven, and the prisoners were in their cells until morning. The guards had turned off TV, and the only sounds were of guys snoring out in the hallway, called "the range," a place between the bars and the windows. A new batch of prisoners came in that afternoon and there weren't enough cells.

"You believe in God, Billy?" Leo stood looking down at Billy. Billy lay on the skinny pad that covered the concrete bunk, arm folded over his eyes.

"No."

"Ever think about it?"

"Used to."

"What'd you think?"

"I don't know, Leo."

"How come you don't believe in God?"

" 'Cause it don't make sense."

"Like because things ain't fair? Like we're here an' all that?"

"No."

"What then?" Leo sat down on the cot beside him. He liked it when the lights were out. He didn't have to look at the babyshit-brown walls or the iron bars, and he could believe for moments at a time they weren't there.

"When I was little, one time when Mom went on the wagon and decided things were gonna be different, she sent me off to Sunday school. And I went a couple of times 'fore I got bored and started cuttin' the classes. Anyways, I remember them talkin' 'bout Jonah and the whale. 'Member hearin' 'bout that?"

"Yeah, the guy rode around inside the whale's stomach and lived to tell about it."

"Well, that's just it, Leo. Couldn't happen."

"Why not? A whale's stomach is a pretty big place, you could probably put in a couch and a TV."

"That's not what happens. What happens is the stomach makes this acid kind of stuff that eats the food. I mean you eat that chicken leg and you chew it all up, but then this acid stuff comes along and eats up the little pieces."

"I never thought about it before," Leo said. "You know, thinking of that, think about this. The ocean must be full of whale shit. How come you never hear about that?"

"Leo, goddammit. Listen for once, will ya? What I'm saying is that Jonah was in there a long time and that acid stuff would have eaten him alive."

"Oh." Leo was quiet for a moment. "Billy, you ever feel like that?"

"Like what?"

"Like you're someplace maybe like in a whale's stomach and you're being eaten alive?"

Now it was Billy's turn to be quiet. Leo went back to his cot. About an hour later Billy said: "Maybe. Sometimes."

EIGHT

"You guys forget Don Ameche invented the telephone? No, you gotta fly, run up my bills." Marty wielded his Mercedes out onto the airport expressway.

"Let's get this straight, Marty," said the well-dressed man riding shotgun. "Compared to our other clients, you run a mom-and-pop, but you make trouble like you're about to take over the Southside of Chicago."

"We didn't take care of your problem, Marty. But somebody did, and that's a problem." The guy in the backseat leaned forward. Marty could smell his breath, he was so close. "Judging by the papers, looks like you got some local muscle to do it for you."

The guys laughed.

"Couple of little muscles," the guy in the front seat said, laughing.

"Little teeny-bopper muscles," the other chimed in, laughing so hard he started choking. "Big-time operation you got here, Marty."

Marty was quiet. He didn't like them being here. Who did they think they were?

"We have one question," said the well-dressed man. "Any way anybody knows anything at all about our relationship, you and I? The kids? They know about you? Know about us?"

"No. Nobody. Just me. Would you get off the kid shit, for God's sake. They didn't do it." He'd said it. It was too late to take it back. Marty shut his eyes for a moment.

"You don't know who did it? But you know the kids didn't do it. That how it is, Marty?" the well-dressed guy asked. "You were at the movies with the kids when it happened? That it?"

"What I mean," Marty said, feeling the perspiration bead up on his forehead and hoping it was too dark in the car for them to see it, "is how could two kids snuff a veteran cop?"

"Marty, Marty, Marty." The guy in the backseat leaned forward. His lips were on Marty's right ear. "You know, we both know, that Puckett was sniffing 'round your place, making it his hangout, right? He pals around with the girls, with your brother-in-law. Your brother-in-law does a little dealing? What's his name? Dierdolf. Dierdorf is a wimp, right? But he does the right thing. Right?"

The guy riding beside Marty handed him a handkerchief.

"Now listen and listen good. If you don't understand something, you ask. Okay? Marty, I want you to guide this Nazi battleship to the Hilton, the one on the Circle. You don't do no business, except the girlie business. No phone calls. You don't talk to your brother-in-law. Nada. We hear our name and your name in the same sentence and one of those little proper nouns come up missing."

Marty dropped them off at the Hilton. He swung back, driving I-70 east, then the northern route on the loop, back toward the club. He turned on public radio. Some great old jazz playing and some great old voice singing about how bananas don't have bones.

Doing a search, even of a one-bedroom apartment, took a long time. Could take days if it were done right. Shanahan normally headed straight for the checkbook and the charge card invoices, but he couldn't help noticing Puckett took great pains with the look of his environment.

Downstairs—after he convinced an elderly lady to let him in because the water main needed investigating—the place looked a little run-down. Broken panes of glass had been indiscriminately replaced with sheet metal, and the willy-nilly selection of chairs in the old lobby hardly reflected the carefully carved woodwork.

Once he picked the lock of Puckett's apartment door, he was surprised to find high-quality, contemporary leather furniture; an impressive, though slightly worn oriental carpet; expensive bookshelves that housed the books of a decidedly literary nature. *The Fire Next Time, Go Tell It on the Mountain, Crime and Punishment, Soul on Ice, Malcolm X, The Color Purple, In Cold Blood, Woman in the Dunes.* There were also several books on South Africa and a few on Eastern religions.

Puckett had read them too. The little creases on the corners of some of the pages indicated where he'd stopped. The last fold was usually somewhere near the end of the book. *The Color Purple* had an inscription. "To Samuel . . ." The rest of the page was ripped out. Not with care, ripped. A smart person would have removed the entire page.

The record collection was eclectic. Chick Corea, Brahms and Beethoven, Prince, some long-haired Japanese musician named Kitaro. The arm of the turntable hovered above a cut on an Elton John album. Shanahan turned on the stereo and lowered the arm to hear Elton singing, "I'm still standing."

A desk folded out of the wall-high shelving. Shanahan flipped on the small but powerful light and went through the papers.

The checkbook revealed little. Car loan, utilities, magazine subscriptions, small monthly checks to Amnesty International, of all places, and CARE. American Express bills revealed a whole lot more. God bless American Express, Shanahan thought. They even provided copies of the signed charge ticket. Nothing but the best for Puckett: $700 suit, $50 shirts, $25 for one pair of underwear. Christ, Shanahan thought, I feel like I'm splurging at two for $7.50.

At least once a week there was an expensive dinner for two. At Fletcher's, Jonathan's Keepe, Château Normandy, Peter's, Sakura. Most of the charges would lead nowhere. He didn't eat often enough at any one place to be known. On the other hand, there was a charge at a florist. If they were delivered, and the recipient didn't turn out to be his mother, he might have something to follow up on.

Was Puckett on the take? Shanahan searched through the drawers for savings account records. One savings account with a $75 balance. Unless he stashed cash somewhere, a safe deposit box maybe, Puckett was living on the edge, financially. Shanahan checked the closet, found a few more file boxes of income tax statements, canceled checks and old bills, amidst several fine suits and an immodest collection of shoes. The bureau drawers held only neatly folded socks and underwear.

Nothing contradicted Shanahan's initial impression that Puckett was on the up and up. He just liked to live in style, and wasn't particularly concerned with his golden years. Good thing.

There were no messages on the answering machine in the bedroom, but he did find two strange pieces of paper. One was half of a ripped photo. All it showed was Puckett in a bathing suit, an ocean and some sailboats behind him. From the set of his shoulder, it looked like the arm that was ripped off when the photo was torn had been around someone. The look on Puckett's face indicated the missing person was probably a woman. That notion was pretty much confirmed by the feminine, light brown hand that remained in the frame. The woman, however, was gone. On the back was written "Barbados, 19 . . ." The rest was on the missing piece.

The other item was a bar napkin from Sweethearts, a go-go bar out on Pendleton Pike. There was something written on the back. Somebody's wet drink had pretty well obliterated the words. He thought he could make out some numbers and a dollar sign.

The kitchen revealed fifths of Meyer's rum and Absolut vodka. Good stuff, Shanahan thought, but they're not bourbon. The refrigerator revealed what you might expect from a bachelor. Very little food. There were five bottles of Sapporo "dry" beer, a liter of Classic Coke, a bottle of tonic water, some leftover sushi in a plastic, carryout container, an opened bottle of Savory and James "fino" sherry, an unopened, round carton of Camembert, and a bottle of dry California wine.

The garbage can was uninspiring. The usual subscription letters, a request from the Quality Paperback Book Club, an unopened Publisher's Clearing House envelope, two eggshells and a butter wrapper.

Shanahan was heading toward the bathroom when he heard someone playing with the lock on the door in the entryway. He wished he'd brought his pistol.

Whoever was poking and scraping at the lock was persistent but hardly accomplished. Shanahan got tired of waiting. He opened the door to find a startled young man on his knees, a spiral notebook on the floor by his knee.

"Two bucks says you're not a locksmith," Shanahan said to the guy who struggled awkwardly to his feet.

"This is Puckett's apartment, isn't it?" the young man asked, face getting redder.

"Yes."

"I'm Puckett's son . . . er, adopted son."

"And I'm Puckett's wife," Shanahan said dryly. "Come in and let's start over."

"I'm Tom English. I work for *Metro Monthly* magazine."

"That's a little more believable."

"Your turn," English said, a little more comfortably.

"Shanahan. I'm investigating Puckett's death."

"I thought that was already decided. Why the investigation?"

Shanahan liked him. English had moved quickly from embarrassment to aggressive questioning. "I had this funny notion that the verdict wasn't in. You know that corny stuff about being innocent until proven guilty."

"Yeah, I know. I know." English seemed tired all of a sudden and let his body sink into the leather cushions on the sofa. "That's the problem. That's one of the many problems."

"Tell me."

"Well first, I've been instructed by my publisher to make the story read 'Good Policeman Killed by Drugged-out Punkers,' or something like that. If that isn't bad enough, I can't get anywhere anyway. Nobody will say anything."

"Poor little reporter. Nobody will talk to you."

"Oh, they'll talk," English said. "Regular chatty Cathys, but they don't say anything."

"Your justification for breaking and entering."

"It's better than yours," English said. "Actually, I didn't break in. You did. You invited me in."

"Okay." Shanahan smiled. "You're right. So who won't spill the beans for you?"

"Nobody. One, I'm young and I have no connections. People *have* to talk to the dailies. They *have* to talk with the TV stations, but they don't have to talk with a snotty-nosed reporter from a city magazine long on style and short on substance. I end up with a lot of P.R. crap. Even the police department gives me nothing. Puckett was a wonderful man, they say."

"He was," Shanahan said. "How 'bout a rum and something. No bourbon."

"What?"

"Let's have a drink and let's talk."

"Wait a minute, why are you being so friendly?"

"I'm a friendly guy."

"Yeah sure. Everybody's a friendly guy. Puckett was a nice, friendly guy."

"That's what I said. He was a nice guy. If he was here right now, he'd offer us a drink. Why don't you go fix me a rum and tonic." He winced. That was Maureen's drink, rum and tonic, twist of lemon. God, he missed her. "Tonic's in the icebox. I'm going to check out the bathroom."

"You checked out the refrigerator?"

"The way to a man's heart . . ."

In the bathroom he found a dozen dried-up, long-stemmed roses, the box they came in, and a card: "Jenny, please, let's talk, Sam." Someone had penned a huge X over the writing. Shanahan's first thought was that Puckett delivered them personally and was rebuffed. But there was a messenger form showing they'd been delivered to him. He had sent them, after all, and they were returned. That means the mysterious Jenny could be traced.

Shanahan opened the medicine cabinet. Nothing in particular. Some Advil, Noxema shave cream, Perry Ellis aftershave, toothpaste, mouthwash. The usual stuff.

"Now, let's talk," Shanahan said, sipping

his drink and settling into the larger of the leather chairs. "First, our young punks didn't do it."

"That's not what I want to hear," English said. "You know, this isn't going too well, so far."

"They're dirty little kids, Leo and Billy. And best I could tell, they didn't change clothes for about four or five days. What they were wearing the night of the murder was what they were wearing when they were arrested."

"Does that mean something?"

"So when you stab somebody in the chest and you just happen to explode the heart in such a way as the blood splatters over everything within ten feet, how is it that Leo and Billy's clothes had no blood on them? Not one drop."

"Christ. That's good," English said.

"Not really. It's pretty circumstantial. Then again, that's what the case is against them. Circumstantial. Nobody can connect the kids with the weapon. They were sloppy enough to leave fingerprints everywhere else, but none were found on the murder weapon. Also circumstantial and pretty weak, but it opens up the possibilities."

"Then who did it?"

"Could be the people he was playing undercover to get. Could be somebody pissed at him for something else. Could be an irate lover by the name of Jenny."

"Jenny? Who's she?"

"That's what you're going to help me find out."

"So now I'm working for you? Why would I do that?"

"Because I'm a brilliant detective, and you, a bright but naive young man, want to learn the art of detection at the feet of the master."

"That's an interesting but not very original theory."

"Or," Shanahan continued, "I can fucking fill you in on the story that could get you a Pulitzer. Quotes from the kids, the defense attorney, what the scene of the crime looks like. And, as the King of Siam once said, 'etcetera, etcetera.' "

"Teach me, master," English said, raising his drink. He took a sip, made a face. "I'm not much of a drinker."

"I feel awfully guilty drinking a dead man's rum," English said. He set his empty glass carefully on the coffee table.

"How about the vodka, then?"

"I mean it," he belched, "the man is dead."

"Some people get happy when they drink, others get sloppy and sentimental, some get angry. You feel guilty. We must do something about that."

"I'm beginning to think you're not a very nice old man," English said.

"You are very observant," Shanahan said. "But look at it this way. In Mr. Puckett's will, how likely is it he would bequeath a half a bottle of rum? I, Samuel Puckett, being of sound mind and body, do hereby bequeath a half bottle of Meyer's rum to my cousin Matilda and her two lovely children."

English giggled. "I see."

"Yes, well, you see this is our sendoff to Samuel Puckett. It's what we Irish do when someone dies."

"But I'm English," he said, then burst into laughter and coughs, crashing back against the sofa. English, slightly intoxicated, was rapidly turning into a downright giddy drunk.

"Very," Shanahan said. "You remember what you're to do tomorrow?"

"Yes, yes, yes. I do. I am to find the mysterious Jenny and then I'm to meet you at Sweethearts at eleven."

"Now, I'll take you home," Shanahan said, sticking the torn picture of Samuel Puckett in his pocket.

"You think I can't drive."

"I said you were observant."

"You're right. But I can't go home like this. Drop me off at the office."

English stumbled through the dark corridors until he came to his little cubicle. He didn't bother with the light in the cube either, simply flicked on his Macintosh. The light from the computer was just enough to illuminate the keyboard.

Appropriate, he thought. The little light in his brain was pretty dim too. He hoped the rum-soaked gray matter wasn't too sloshy. He didn't have to make a whole helluva lot of sense; but he had to get some of the things Shanahan told him in the car into the more reliable brain of the computer.

He began to type:

> Private Detective. Elderly man named Shanahan. Fact: Puckett stabbed in heart. Blood everywhere. NOT on kid's

clothes. Mystery woman: Jenny somebody. Lover? Possible motive: Broken heart. Something to do with Eastside go-go bar. Sweethearts. Leo's girlfriend: Some girl named Lisa, hangs out at their digs in an abandoned house near the corner of Michigan and Dearborn.

It seemed to take hours to type just these few short notes. He closed out "document," pressed the little square that said "save." He shut off the computer.

He'd do this right, he told himself. And if Connell didn't like it, he could go fuck himself. English would get the story published elsewhere. He missed Sarah. Fourteen years at the magazine, and in a few short minutes she was gone. No good-bye parties, no long lunches to talk about her future. Just gone.

Would serve Connell right if he took the story to the dailies. No more interviews with the governor's wife or the happy TV news anchorperson. He was pretty sure he could live without another famous haunted-house story for the October issue. Maybe he could be the crime reporter for the *Star* or the *News*, or maybe that new publication, whatever it was.

That was the last thing he thought about, until Paul, the magazine's ever-bubbling art director, shook his shoulder.

"I take it the wrinkled look is in," said the redhead all too cheerfully. "Connell's in his office, kiddo. Good thing you're not shaving yet."

"Thanks, Paul," English said.

"Mrs. Connell was in too."

"Mrs. Connell? Here? That's a first, isn't it?"

"Yes, very much a first. She was leaving when I came in. He came in about fifteen minutes later."

"What did she want?" English said, though with his headache, he wasn't sure he cared.

"Don't know. She looked at me like she'd just turned on the lights and found a roach in her sink. By the way, I've got some mouthwash back in my cube?" He scampered off. "Toodles," he shouted.

"Toodles," English said without conviction.

NINE

Connell didn't like how the evening had gone last night. First, having to deal with a cub reporter like English; second, watching Sarah Mundy give him the "I'm going to get you for this" eye: and then two hours with a bunch of jackasses at the club. The local business weekly had just come out with the "ten most powerful people in the city." Connell had failed for the first time in five years to be in the top ten.

Whenever Connell wasn't on one of those lists, *Forbes,* or *Fortune,* he'd pretty much dismiss the lists as being "made-up." He'd do this for himself and for anyone with whom he could casually interject his opinions. Now Connell was even off the city lists. It was humiliating.

"No one knows who hides what assets," he said, smiling to Harvey Bamberger. "It's all in how you count the beans."

"And if you can find all the beans to count?" Bamberger added, nudging a small smile from Connell's thin lips.

"Exactly," Connell said.

It wouldn't have disturbed him so much had it not been that over the past five years he'd suffered some pretty big losses, which he had more than made up for, but couldn't show on the books. Nor could he explain to Bamberger or to anyone else for that matter. Not even his wife. It was troubling because in the heart of hearts of Connell types, the number of figures before the decimal point was like the batting average of a baseball player. It was a form of measurement everyone who counted—and many who didn't—used to keep score.

After chatting with Bamberger and the boys, he spent four hours in the Red Roof Inn on the Eastside, mixing business with pleasure. Both were usually good, but there was a kind of shrillness in her voice these days, a demanding tone. He remembered seeing a movie once with that Englishman, Laurence Harvey, about a man who fell in love with this horrible woman, and Connell felt a little like the Englishman.

He should dump her. No question. He tried to imagine taking her to one of those dinners where they sat at the dais and discussed international affairs. Connell would, on one hand, be envied, but publicly he'd be the laughingstock in every club, board room, and charity dinner in the city.

His wife was a little rough at first too, but it was excused because they were young and because they hadn't achieved the status then, except by way of being James A Connell, Sr.'s son. But his wife grew into it. He wasn't Connell senior's son anymore except to a few old-timers, and he no longer had youth on his side.

There was no future in this extramarital relationship either, but she did things for him his wife would never do. So she had him two ways. There was the business thing. And there was this sex thing. He had divided them in his mind that way. As long as it didn't get any more complicated than that, he could handle it.

Connell put last night out of his mind and went down the stairs and into the kitchen. Maribel had his coffee and plain toast as she always did. Connell believed you could set a clock by her actions. She arrived every day at seven-thirty A.M. by taking the bus and then walking the mile and a half from the stop. In all the years, Maribel had never caused the Connells any trouble. No children problems. No health problems. And the only days she missed were her mother's funeral and two days during the blizzard a couple of years ago. And nothing ever came up missing.

She was a sometime cook, sometime housekeeper, human message center for the household, part-time nanny when the kids were young. A young mulatto woman, Maribel was hired by Connell's father five years before his death. She was in fact the granddaughter of the woman who had kept house for the Connells for thirty years, a woman who helped raise Jim and his sister Jessica.

He laughed getting into his Mercedes. Maribel rarely said anything out of line. But he did remember her asking him an embarrassing question once.

"How come, Mr. Connell," she said, straight-faced, "with all your money, you buy such cheap shoes?"

It was the same thing he was asked last night, after the dinner at the club, when he met her. It was what started the argument.

What a mouth, Connell thought, driving down the long drive. He laughed again, remembering how she used her mouth to make up with him as he drove her to her car. He wanted to be with her right now. He turned up the volume on his stereo.

"The cheap bitch," he said, thinking that nothing good would come of it, any of it, anything that had to do with her. That wouldn't stop him and he knew it.

The foul taste in his mouth was familiar. The headache wasn't. Shanahan had been drunk before. Not all that long ago. But he hadn't had a hangover since Paris. Thirty, forty years ago. Burgundy then. Rum now.

Einstein sat on the nightstand next to the bed, giving that look, as if he'd brought Shanahan unwillingly to consciousness with the mere power of his unrelenting stare.

"Shut up," he said to the cat, who hadn't uttered a sound and wasn't even breathing hard. Hearing a human voice, Casey bounded in the room, doing his "I've got to pee" dance. His bark pierced Shanahan's swollen brain. Einstein hopped on the bed. Casey barked louder. With difficulty, Shanahan tried to focus on the blue digits of his clock radio. Finally, he could make it out as if he were looking through a fog: 9:47.

He slipped on his pants and followed Casey to the door, let him out, went to the kitchen, opened a can of Nine Lives. Einstein paced impatiently across the counter, gobbled the food.

"Never, never rum," Shanahan told Einstein. He went into the bathroom, found a plastic container marked Excedrin. The cap wouldn't come off. He went back into the kitchen and, with a steak knife, sawed the bottle at the neck and extracted three of the little pills, threw them into his mouth and gulped water directly from the faucet.

"Damn." Something flickered in his brain. Slowly, the flicker died, leaving a vague, nagging question. Something he had to do. "Damn, damn, damn, damn," he said. Court at eleven. The kids were being arraigned. "They'll run late," he reassured himself.

He dressed, this time wearing his black suit. For some reason he wanted to look especially respectable. Why? The press maybe. Msss. Bailey maybe. Maybe Maureen. She was due in today. He didn't want to look as bad as he felt.

He almost left despite the phone call.

"Yes," he said into the phone. His voice still wasn't at full strength.

"Mr. Shanahan?"

"Maybe."

"It's Tom."

"Tom who?"

"English." The voice sounded hurt.

"Yes, English. Listen, I've got to run."

"I know, that's why I called. I can't make it to the courthouse and I'm depending on you."

"I'm not feeling particularly dependable."

"I found the lover."

"What lover?" Shanahan knew he should know what English was referring to, but the mind only hovered near consciousness.

"Puckett's lover, the great florist connection? Remember?" English said.

"Tell me tonight. At Sweethearts, right?" Shanahan heard English's protests as he lowered the telephone toward its cradle.

"Shanahan, wait!"

"What?" he asked impatiently.

"I've got to tell you," English said, and then whispered a name. Shanahan was stunned, and he was clearly in no mood for getting stunned.

"You don't say," Shanahan said.

"I do," English said smugly. "I do indeed."

"Come over to the house tonight," Marty said, a telephone in his ear, and looking out of place in his wife's pink and mauve bedroom. "Early dinner and then to the club." Everything was distasteful. The cigar, the cold cup of coffee, the phone conversation. He should've gone back to his own room last night. The colors in her bedroom made him nauseous in the daytime.

"How the hell do I know what she's fixing? Chicken probably. It's always chicken. Helen doesn't know how to fix anything else." He hung up.

He crawled out of bed, glanced at his pudgy, gray-haired head and avalanche of a body in the mirror. "Your sister and her brilliant choice for eternity are coming to dinner," he shouted in the general direction of the hallway.

"Don't yell. How many times I tell you not to yell." Helen came into the room. "Get your clothes on, will you."

"What? Who's gonna see?"

"I'm seeing, Marty, I'm seeing. And it's disgusting."

"It's my fuckin' house, Helen." He was about to tell her that there were plenty of chicks at the club who'd be happy to take her place. But she'd already gone.

Marty went to the bathroom, put on his robe and went into the kitchen. "Sorry,

Helen. Your brother-in-law gets me all worked up." What he wanted to tell her was that the guy who married her sister was so stupid he'd offed a cop, that because of that the guy her sister married was gonna get offed, and that he wasn't sure he was too sad about the idea. He just hoped he wasn't in contention for getting offed himself. He took a glass from the cupboard and put it by the orange juice pitcher.

"Yeah, why don't you give it up?" She put the pitcher in the refrigerator without pouring him a glass. "You never stop with him. Why don't you fire him?" She put a plate of dry food down for twin Abyssinian cats, cats who intimidated Marty. "I'll tell you why. 'Cause nobody else would put up with your crap. That's why. And furthermore, Mr. Homeowner, the 'fucking house' is half mine. So are the fucking cars and the fucking bank accounts!"

Marty smiled. He liked her independent, angry, liked the fire in her eyes. Ten years ago she could've been in *Playboy.* She was still better-looking than any of the girls on Sweethearts' runway.

Helen went to the refrigerator, reached for the orange juice. "Just don't take me for granted, Marty." She poured him a glass. "With what I know, I can put you away for a hundred years, while I relax away the hours on a beach in the south of France."

Marty nodded toward the cats. "Don't forget to take Fred and Ethyl with you."

"You never stop needling, do you, Marty?"

"Send me a postcard from the Riviera, sweetie!"

He took his orange juice with him. To *his* bathroom—the one with the deep green tile and the mahogany-colored towels. He laid his orange juice glass and cigar on the sink, turned the water on in the shower, looked in the mirror. He remembered when he used to worry about his looks.

Shanahan knew the judge. Not personally. He'd seen him on a number of occasions, most notably at his own divorce proceedings. Years ago, back when divorces were real occasions. The judge was a crackpot then, and there was no sign he was about to relinquish his time in the spotlight now that he was a criminal judge.

He badgered the little man, who was not only up on charges of violating a restraining order, but on criminal charges because he'd thrown a brick through the window of his wife's sister's car. The little man shook with anger in a tan trench coat so large it fit him like a wet grocery sack. The estranged wife, a large woman, had an operatic presence, proud and comic. She stood, hands on hips and aiming her substantial bosom at her husband, while the judge seemed to be playing his own game of target in a shooting gallery. His head weaved back and forth and up and down, a black-robed Groucho Marx, doing his best to disrupt the court from behind the towering blond desk.

Shanahan looked around the court. Leo and Billy were being led in from the holding cells. They wore blue coveralls with bright yellow, stenciled lettering: JAIL. They sat on a bench to the right and behind the judge, guarded by a county sheriff. Ms. Bailey sat two rows in front of Shanahan. He recognized no one else.

Suddenly, the judge's eyes lifted and focused on something at the rear of the court. He sobered and all eyes turned toward the back. There was a moment of quiet as Robert Silvers, the newsmaking city prosecutor himself strode up the aisle, looking both self-conscious and disturbed.

Shanahan turned back toward the front

in time to see the defendant in the trench coat pull out a revolver. The first shot, aimed at the judge, might have hit him. Maybe not. But the judge's head was no longer visible, and a series of shots, all sounding like they came from a cap pistol, downed the wife and her attorney.

Both the bailiff and the sheriffs deputy had the little man—now limp as a washcloth—subdued before the crowd of reporters and attorneys surrounded them. Most of the onlookers squeezed through the rear doors of the courtroom.

Shanahan stood. His eyes went to the little corner to the right and behind the judge's bench, to the plain bench next to the chicken-wire, reinforced glass door. Empty. No sign of Billy and Leo. Shanahan jerked around to the rear of the courtroom, just in time to see Leo's blond head disappear.

He turned forward again to look into Ms. Bailey's shocked, wide-eyed gaze.

TEN

Shanahan wanted to talk to Jennifer Bailey. He was about to approach her and suggest they go sit somewhere, have a cup of coffee and chat. Instead, he decided to follow her. It was a hunch, and as it turned out, not a particularly good one.

The hallway was packed with people, many of them bumping into each other. "How'd the guy have a gun? There are metal detectors." Shanahan heard two lawyers talking. "Maybe a plastic gun. Who knows?" A swarm of policemen broke up the conversation as they penetrated the civilian crowd.

Outside, traffic was a mess. Police and county sheriffs everywhere. SWAT teams, police in cars, on motorcycles, on horseback. Traffic was gridlocked. All looking for Billy and Leo.

He had managed to follow the attorney to the parking garage, watch her get into a red BMW. But they were separated in the snarl of traffic, the searches and general confusion. The best bet seemed to be her office. That's where he found her, calmly though curtly taking a male secretary through a list of things to do.

"I'm afraid, considering the circumstances, there isn't a terrible lot to say to you, Mr. Shanahan."

"On the contrary, Ms. Bailey, there's quite a bit to talk about."

"Let me put it another way, then." She took a deep breath. "Now is not a convenient time for me." That was to be Shanahan's dismissal. She turned toward her employee. "Steve, would you make three copies of the Lucas letter—"

"I plan to stay and ask some questions, and I think you might prefer doing that in your office," Shanahan said.

The secretary looked quickly at Shanahan, then just as quickly at his boss. It was apparent to Shanahan that Steve had never witnessed anyone refusing an order from her, direct or implied.

Her eyes shut; one long, frustrated blink. When they opened, she smiled coolly. "Steve, why don't you get started, and we'll finish after I've had a chance to dispose of Mr. Shanahan."

Shanahan followed her into the office.

He shut the door behind him and couldn't hold back the laughter. "Dispose?"

"A legal phrase." Even though she stood with her arms stubbornly crossed over her chest, there was a genuine grin on her face. "As in dispose of a case, not as in dispose of a body."

"That makes me feel more comfortable. You might want to sit down, Ms. Bailey."

"No thank you. I intend this to be brief. So please, get to the point."

"What prompted you to take this case?"

She looked puzzled. "What do you mean?"

"We're starting with an easy question. They're going to get harder."

"Mr. Shanahan, sometimes I make more money in one day than families where I come from make in a year. I'm sure you've heard of *pro bono.* By taking a few cases like Leonard and William's, it helps me reduce the level of my newly found middle-class guilt."

"Helping the poor?"

"Yes."

"Why two little white kids? On the whole, there are probably more black kids victimized by the system."

"I don't understand this line of questioning."

"I think it's even more peculiar you would volunteer to defend someone accused of killing a black man."

"Are you trying to say that one of us is a racist, Mr. Shanahan?"

"Maybe worse."

"What could be worse, Mr. Shanahan? Tell me what could be worse."

"Defending the alleged murderers of your lover."

She was quiet. Shanahan continued. "You went to his apartment, after his death, and removed everything that made you a part of his life. You shouldn't have sent back the flowers. Or, at least you should have checked the wilted bouquet in the bathroom wastebasket."

Jennifer Bailey sighed and went to her desk to sit down. The phone buzzed. It was Steve's voice. "Ms. Bailey, it's time for me to go home. Would you like for me to stick around for a while? It's all right."

"No," she said absently. "No, please go on home. We'll talk in the morning." She pressed a button on the phone and looked up at Shanahan.

"Sam was seeing someone else. And I

hated him for it. He said it was all part of what he was working on. 'Work' he said."

"Who was he seeing?"

"I don't know."

"You know nothing about her?"

"She was white. She was a little older than he was. She was married, and I gather she had money."

"You didn't hire one of your competent investigative services to check it out?"

"No. This is my personal life. And quite frankly, Mr. Shanahan, I'm not sure any of this is your business either."

"Well, let's look at it objectively. You have a motive."

"Yes, classic, isn't it?" She almost laughed.

"You broke into his . . ."

"I had a key."

". . . apartment and tampered—that's a mild phrase—with evidence."

"It's not tampering. It had nothing to do with his death. But it had a lot to do with my life. I didn't want to be part of the inevitable investigation. I didn't want my name splattered all over the newspapers. I worked hard to get where I am. I don't intend to lose it to the media."

"If I were a lawyer and I killed someone

and then the police arrested the wrong person, I'd certainly like to be the defense attorney. Wouldn't you?"

Her hands went to her temples and she groaned: "Oh my God."

"A good defense attorney could do more to get these kids convicted than a staff of prosecuting attorneys. Case closed. Jealous lover never even investigated, let alone prosecuted."

Shanahan went to the window, pulled aside the heavy drapery, looked out on the city below. It was back to normal. Giant cranes pulling steel from muddy holes. He wondered if the police had found Leo and Billy. Wondered if they were still alive.

"The reason I decided to defend them," Jennifer Bailey said, speaking softly but choosing her words carefully, "was that I believe, more than I believe anything in life, that they didn't do it. I wasn't about to let some underpaid, inexperienced, court-appointed attorney lose and therefore close the case."

"Why do you believe their innocence so strongly?"

"I loved him. That's the first thing you have to understand, Mr. Shanahan. Otherwise I wouldn't have hated him so much. Does that make sense?"

"Yes. But as the lawyers on TV say, please answer the question."

"I'm getting to it. We were right for each other. What I felt was a petty, childish rage. We would have gotten back together and we would have lived out our lives . . . together. I loved him, and I loved him because I knew him. I knew him very well. Mr. Shanahan, he could have handled a couple of teenage burglars. He was on to something much more significant, more sinister, more dangerous than Billy and Leo. And that, not a couple of children, is what killed him."

"Okay."

"Do you believe me, Mr. Shanahan?"

"Can't say as I can answer that question, Ms. Bailey. I don't believe they did it. And frankly, I'm a little short on suspects."

Maureen's car was in the driveway. So was a pearl-black Acura Legend, engine running. Shanahan had also passed a red two-door Caddy with a white fabric top parked a half block away. The driver turned away as he went by. Because of the dusk and the rain, Shanahan couldn't make out anything. Man, woman, young, old, nothing.

Busy place, Shanahan thought. He knew the Acura but he didn't know the Caddy. Maybe the two came together. Maybe not. Shanahan parked his Malibu in front of the house. He could see the back of the man's head as he approached the Acura. An irate husband? No doubt. Shanahan was pretty sure he knew just which irate husband it was. What he didn't know was whether it was safe to approach him.

Shanahan tapped on the window. The man turned, startled. It was the same man, Mr. Dunfy, whom he had seen coming out of the girl's apartment. The automatic window slid quietly down.

"Mr. Shanahan, my name is Dunfy, but I suspect you already know that." His voice was without emotion. "My wife hired you to find out how I spent my evenings."

"Yes," Shanahan said, waiting. The air was cold. He saw his breath puffing out in front of his words.

"I've convinced my wife you are a charlatan," he said, voice still well-modulated.

"Bully for you."

"She intends not to pay you, of course."

"Oh, of course, Mr. Dunfy. You just

don't pay charlatans, it just encourages them."

"However, whether or not I treat an attractive young woman for a severe case of depression is of no consequence to either you or my wife."

"Yes, of course, no consequence," Shanahan said, wishing the man would come to the point. He wanted to talk to Maureen before she finished packing her suitcase.

"But then, you must be paid for your time . . ." He pulled an envelope from his pocket.

"That is logical, Mr. Dunfy. I'd say you are on the right track there."

"You'll find a thousand dollars. That should take care of your time plus a little for your understanding."

Shanahan took the envelope. "I think my bill was about eight hundred. Two hundred a day—four days."

"My appreciation, then," Mr. Dunfy said.

The window quietly closed, ending the conversation, and Mr. Dunfy backed to the end of the driveway, paused. He looked back, both ways, and pulled out, gliding out down the street.

Shanahan looked through the window of the door. He could see Maureen sitting on the overstuffed chair, arms folded in her lap, staring straight ahead. When he opened the door, she turned, looked at him, a strange smile crossing her lips.

"Hi, Shanahan," she said. The phone was ringing.

"Hi yourself," he said, walking into the room, seeing Billy and Leo sitting on the sofa. Leo stood up. He was breathing heavily. Billy held Shanahan's own .45, held it calmly, turning the gun from Maureen to the detective.

"Hi kids," Shanahan said as he continued toward the phone. "You mind, it's driving me crazy?"

Billy reasserted his ownership of the gun, and Shanahan answered the phone.

"Yep," he said into the receiver. There was a long pause. He looked around the room. Maureen smiled at him again. He smiled back. "Lieutenant Rafferty . . . yes, well then, I'll send you the bill. You have a particular restaurant you want me to send it to?"

Shanahan hung up the phone. "Everything happens at once, you know how that is? I'm off your case. Fired. So can I get you kids some milk and cookies before you go?"

"You gonna take that, Billy?" Leo blustered. Billy smiled, laid the gun on the table next to the sofa.

"I leave you alone for a couple of days . . ." Maureen said with resignation but not without humor.

"Yeah, I know." Shanahan walked over to the table, picked up the gun, showed Leo the hole in the handle where a clip would be if it were loaded. "Not loaded, Leo." He put it in the desk drawer. "You staying here tonight?" he asked Maureen.

"I wouldn't miss whatever this is for the world." She cracked a smile.

"What are you going to do?" Leo asked nervously.

"Order a pizza. You like pizza?" Maureen asked. "I haven't had anything to eat since breakfast."

"No anchovies," Billy said calmly. Leo looked confused.

"About ten," Shanahan said to Maureen, "I've got to go down to some club on Pendleton Pike and watch girls take their clothes off. You want to come along?"

"You got a hot date?" Maureen asked.

"With a young reporter."

"Pretty?"

"He's kinda cute," Shanahan said, "but I wouldn't call him pretty."

ELEVEN

Shanahan went to the back door to see why Casey was barking. He called but the dog wouldn't come. He went out and found a man in a blue uniform standing behind the chain-link fence. He held a .38.

"Casey, you're being foolish. The nice man has a pistol."

"Call off your dog or he's dead," the guy said.

"Sit, Casey!" Shanahan ordered. "He doesn't like guns, and I'm not too fond of them myself." Shanahan opened the gate, admonished Casey to "stay" and led the officer into the living room from the back.

There were two other policemen, one in uniform and another, a younger man with a haircut like a Marine, in a dark suit.

"I thought it was the pizza," Maureen said, shrugging her shoulders.

"I hope you guys brought the beer," Shanahan said to the younger cop.

"You won't have time to drink it, Mr. Shanahan," said the short-haired man in the suit, who now offered Shanahan a look at his badge. "Harboring fugitives? My name is Lieutenant Swann, Matthew Swann. Two N's. And I think I need to take you all in."

"They didn't harbor nobody," Billy said. He hadn't bothered to stand up, instead remained seated at the desk with his feet up.

"They give out law degrees at the state farm?" the lieutenant asked calmly.

"We wouldn't let 'em call."

"Oh, I see," the cop said, "you held 'em captive with your baby blues?"

Billy pulled up Shanahan's .45. Aimed it between the officer's eyes.

"Shit!" Leo said.

"You're a half second away from being terminal, kid," Swann said calmly. But the fact was, the police did not have their weapons drawn.

"Save on the electric bill," Billy said, his voice calm. Suddenly he let the automatic twirl down on his trigger finger and offered it to the cop. One of the uniformed cops walked over and took it.

"You're lucky, kid," the young officer said.

"I'd say you're a lucky cop," Billy said, brushing the hair back from his eyes. "I had nothing to lose. You were about to lose your mind, and a mind is a terrible thing to waste. Billy stayed cool. So did the young cop in civvies. He smiled a kind of sad smile as he nodded toward the two uniformed officers.

"Let's go," the young lieutenant said as the handcuffs were placed on Billy and Leo. Shanahan, surprised by their professionalism—no roughing up—followed them to the door. Outside, there were fifteen police cars in the middle of the street.

"Wow," Leo said, "look at that." He looked back at Shanahan, his awed expression shrinking to worry. "You still going to help us?"

Shanahan nodded. He stepped outside. He saw the Domino Pizza car half a block away. The red Caddy was gone. Who did it belong to? Who wanted the kids back in the slammer?

Marty took a final swill of wine. Helen and her sister were talking about the shops on Worth Avenue in Palm Springs. "C'mon,

Dorf, let's get some good stuff and go out by the pool." Marty put his hand on his brother-in-law's shoulder.

"Okay by me," Dorf said, unaccustomed to Marty making such a friendly gesture. "But you already drained the pool, didn't you?"

"Yeah, we're gonna go look at a big hole, Dorf. A hole big enough to bury the both of us."

The chubby guy who married Marty's sister had a laugh like a pig. Snort, snort. He held out his glass as Marty filled it, then followed Marty outside.

It was cool. Marty reached in his jacket pocket and pulled out two U.S. Air tickets. "Tonight you go to the Hyatt Hotel. Tomorrow morning you go to the airport. You get on a plane for Orlando. In Orlando, you change planes for Key West."

"What's this, Marty?"

"You just won a free trip to the destination of my choice. I got reservations for you and your lovely spouse at a guest lodge. Okay? It's all written down."

"This is all really nice, Marty, but—"

"There's five thousand in with the tickets. Don't go home and pack. Don't call anybody."

"What about the dog? What about Chiquita?"

"Helen will take care of Chiquita. We'll bring Chiquita over here and pray the cats don't eat her."

"What's this all about?" Dorf was beginning to whine.

"Well, when you waste a guy, sometimes there's some other guy who wants to waste you." Marty was half enjoying himself. "And for you, Dorf, there's two guys in Valentino suits who think you talk too much."

"Hey, Marty, you're kidding, right? This is ridiculous!"

"Listen, Dorf, lightning struck my uncle Joe. My aunt Edith walks out by the barn and sees his body smoking and smelling like a well-done Kansas City strip. That's fucking ridiculous. This isn't ridiculous. It makes perfect sense. What you think? You kill a guy and you think that everything's gonna be all right after they roll the credits and you walk out to your car?"

"Marty, I gotta tell you. You know me. I'm a prize schnook. I like my big Lincoln Town Car, right? I get a house, I have to starve to make the mortgage payments. I talk big. I know nobody buys it. Everybody knows I'm a schnook, but I get to feel good for a while. I was just trying to make you think I was a tough guy, like I was worth it to you."

"Yeah, well, being a tough guy is one thing. Talking like a tough guy and pulling some stupid stunt just might get us both killed. But right now, I think it's you they want."

"What I'm trying to tell you, Marty. I made it all up. I didn't kill Puckett."

"Save it."

"It's true, Marty. You gotta tell 'em." Marty turned and walked back toward the house. "It seemed so easy, Marty. I read it in the papers. The kids were going down for it. Who would know?"

Marty stopped. He believed Dorf, and he also despised him more than if he'd done it.

"You know what you're gonna do in Key West? You're gonna sit on your fat ass and the sun is gonna squeeze the sweat out of you. Sweat's gonna spew out of you like juice from an orange in a strong fist. You're not gonna want to do nothin' but sit, and it all comes out, down your forehead, into your eyes, down the bridge of your nose like you're melting. But the thing is, you're doing nothin', just sittin' and sweatin'. The place is gonna squeeze you dry."

"I leave you alone for a few weeks and you're in trouble," Maureen said. The street lamps weren't bright on that stretch of Washington Street as the car headed east toward the Interstate 465 loop. Shanahan couldn't tell if she was smiling.

"I hope your father gets better."

"I don't think he will," she said. She told him her sister was watching him for a few days so she could come up and get some things washed, get a little rest.

There was a long silence. At the intersection where he'd pulled the car to a stop, the lights were brighter. He could see her face. Untelling.

"The little punks are in trouble," she said.

"Deep," Shanahan said. He told her the story.

"So you *were* going to harbor two fugitives?"

Shanahan turned off the interstate at the Pendleton Pike exit. They'd be at Sweethearts in just a few minutes.

"I have a hard time seeing them as escaped convicts."

"But they are, aren't they?" She didn't sound worried.

"I guess."

"What was the call from Rafferty about?" she asked. "He call off your investigation?"

Shanahan nodded. "Gettin' too rough for him. You want to spend some time away until this thing gets cleared up?" Shanahan asked.

"Do you want me to?"

"No. I didn't want to spend the last several days—"

"Thanks," she interrupted him, leaned up, kissed him on the cheek.

"I'd have come down."

"I know. There were a lot of things going on. In my mind. I had to be alone with him."

She waited for Shanahan to say something. The faint drizzle had accumulated on the window. He turned on the wipers.

"It may not make any sense. Dad can't say anything. I don't think he knows I'm there," she said matter-of-factly, "but I had to be with him. I had to think about things."

Shanahan guided the car into the crowded parking lot. Instead of choosing the closest spot, he parked near the exit, backed the car in. He turned off the lights, the ignition.

"Things?" he asked.

"Things," she said. It was clear to Shanahan he was not to inquire further.

"Okay," he said.

"Now let's go inside and see if these girls know how to take their clothes off."

Just as they were about to enter, Shanahan saw a red Caddy with a white top pull into the parking lot. He turned, caught the full blast of the headlights in his eyes. The car passed them quickly, too quickly for him to get a make on the driver, and still adjusting to the flash in his eyes, he couldn't focus on the license plate. The car made a quick turn and was back out on the street.

"Damn," Shanahan said.

"What?"

"I wanted the plate number."

"Flat twelve," Maureen said.

"Flat twelve? What the hell is that?"

"That's what the plate said."

"You see the driver?"

"No."

"Man or woman?"

"I couldn't tell. Rain on the glass. What do you want anyway, Shanahan? I got the plate number. Don't I get a junior g-man badge?"

He put his arm around her. "Something. Something more than that." He kissed her on the cheek. "Bless you my child, for you may have just solved a murder."

"You're kidding."

The place was familiar. Go-go saloons were about as different from each other as two Baptist churches. Sweethearts fit the cliché. Lots of red neon, lots of brass. Lots of mirrors. And a D.J. who knew just what heavy bass numbers to pick from last year's Top Forty.

"Why don't you go on in," Shanahan told Maureen. "Somewhere in that din there's a kid sitting by himself. Name's English. Strike up a friendship."

The public telephone was down the entry hall on the way to the men's room, next to the cigarette machine.

He plunked a quarter in the slot. He had a brief conversation, then hung up and plunked another quarter in.

"Hello?" came Rafferty's weary voice on the other end.

"Shanahan."

"The check's in the mail," Rafferty said.

"That's not what I'm calling about."

"Good, because the check isn't in the mail," Rafferty said. "How'd you get my home phone?"

"The mayor gave it to me."

"You called Edie. Listen, you're off the case."

"Yeah, well, I need you to run a plate for me."

"You don't listen. Shanahan, you're off the case, give it up."

"It's a custom plate. Red Caddy. Probably an 'eighty-six. The plate says, Flat twelve. It's somehow involved in all of this."

"No shit," Rafferty said sarcastically.

"What's that supposed to mean?"

"Well, my incompetent P.I., the red Caddy is definitely involved in the case."

"Well, my little asshole lieutenant, give me the goods or I'll serve you up to every TV station in town."

"Figure out the handle, yourself Flat twelve. What does 'twelve' mean to you?"

"Puberty, for all I know, would you—"

"What does twelve inches mean to you?"

"I don't want to hazard a . . . oh shit . . . a foot. Flatfoot. Cop. All right, you've had your fun with riddles. You guys got a cop on me?"

Rafferty laughed. "Call in the Ghost-busters. That's Puckett's car."

It took Shanahan a moment to recover. He figured the driver to be the murderer, not the murderee. "So who's driving it?"

"Whoever has the key, I guess."

"That's the first good answer you've given me." Shanahan hung up.

TWELVE

Marty was sure he heard the glass breaking and felt the floor move beneath him before he heard the sound. But there was no mistaking the sound. He moved cautiously to the living room, hearing the roar of the fire and Helen's screams. He knew they had to be loud, but they were muffled compared to the sound of his heart beating.

"Don't go out there!" he yelled, jerking Helen back so hard she fell, cutting her legs and arms on the glass.

Then all he heard was the cracking, sucking sounds of the fire. He felt the heat on his chest. It took a few minutes to find his pulse. He felt his heart. When he did, he called the police.

"Can I buy you two a drink?" Shanahan shouted above a Tina Turner song.

"If you're trying to pick me up, I already have a date," Maureen said, holding Tom in his seat by putting her hand on Tom's shoulder.

"Home wrecker," Shanahan said to Tom. He sat down in front of the glass of whiskey Maureen had ordered.

"Our friend here is taking his cola straight," Maureen said. Tom looked at Shanahan expectantly.

"Hate to spoil good cola with something like whiskey or rum. Big day, English."

"Maureen told me about Leo and Billy. What about the lawyer, Jennifer what's-her-name?"

"Bailey. Jennifer Bailey says she didn't kill him," Shanahan said.

"You believe her?" English asked, stealing glances at the pretty young Asian girl on stage.

"You talking about the girl up there twirling her—"

"Jennifer," English insisted.

"I was inclined to believe her until I found out that the red Caddy with the vanilla top that was parked outside my humble abode belongs to a dead guy named Puckett."

"What?" English said.

"You found out already? You're quick, Shanahan," Maureen said, "but you couldn't have done it without me."

"True."

"Puckett's dead," English said. "Also true," Shanahan said.

"Then who . . ." English said slowly, finally finishing with, "Jennifer?"

"It's not unlikely that she would have a spare set of keys or know where to find his car."

"She did it, then," Maureen added.

"Not necessarily true. That's a pretty wild stunt for a conservative woman like Jennifer Bailey, especially after our conversation."

"Is she pretty?" Maureen asked.

"Who?"

"Jennifer Bailey."

"Strangely so," Shanahan volunteered. "Anyway, the murderer could have found the keys on Puckett's body. The only thing it shows is that the murderer wasn't some surprise intruder. He had to know Puckett—at least well enough to know what kind of car he drove."

"He could have seen Puckett drive up.

After he killed him, he could have taken the keys?" Maureen raised one eyebrow in triumph.

"Sexist!" Shanahan said to her. "Why does the murderer have to be a 'he'?"

"Same reason cats are female and dogs are male until you learn otherwise. The French are pretty good about things having genders." English rose to her defense.

"Thing is, it's not likely that he would be driving his own car on the stakeout, especially not with custom plates that said "Flat twelve."

Both Shanahan and English looked up to the stage.

"Why are we here?" Maureen asked. "Do detectives do a better job solving mysteries in the presence of naked women? Or is it an image thing?"

"We're here to do detective stuff," Shanahan said, smiling. "Puckett had a connection here of some sort. Maybe with the owner or bartender or one of the dancers. I'm here to talk with English, keep him informed for his Pulitzer Prize–winning story. Then I expect I'll pick up a dancer."

"Say what?" Maureen said.

"Unless English wants to do it."

The pretty Asian girl left the stage after

showing some unique ways to pick up tips from the gents in the seats next to the runway. An older, more experienced dancer emerged to a Rolling Stones blues number.

"You'll do no such thing. Besides, Tom is more attractive."

"Thanks," Shanahan said dryly. "You have an expense account, English?"

"Oh, I can see that on my expense report. Connell would have my balls." Suddenly he looked at Maureen. "Sorry."

Maureen laughed.

"Don't worry English, she talks like a—" He stopped short.

"A what?" Maureen asked.

"A worldly woman," Shanahan said quickly, then turned to English. "Your flesh might be willing, but it's the mind that has to work. No offense to your reporting skills, but this line of questioning is better left to me."

"Listen to him, will ya?" Maureen said. "He's gone from two hundred a day to James Bond."

"I really don't want them to know I'm asking." Shanahan blushed. "But . . . to make you happy, I'll be buying time and information only." Maureen raised her other eyebrow. "I promise." He turned to

English. "Would you drop Maureen off at my place?"

"Sure," English said. "Let me use the john first, okay?"

"So when the snake died, I said, 'Thank you, Jesus,' 'cause I never really cared about him anyway." The dancer was older than she appeared on stage, and Shanahan, who now followed her up the gold-carpeted stairway to her apartment, was convinced she had to be older than Maureen and not nearly as attractive.

"I spent some time with a revival and was cured fifty-seven times for lower back pain. Only I don't think out of the fifty-seven times it ever worked." Sally was going to have a voice like Selma Diamond if she continued with the cigarettes. "I've danced in Miami and Phoenix. I started in Vegas, honey. Now that was class."

Her living room was tidy. The lack of personal possessions made Shanahan think of a motel room. He wondered if this was a common retreat or whether she actually lived here.

"Not much of me here, is there?" she asked, as if she were psychic. "Honey, I travel so much, I've got a box of sentimental junk stored in Louisville and I dumped the rest. Get you a drink? All I have is beer." She went through a pair of swinging doors, presumably to the kitchen. "The bath is right down that hall, make yourself comfy."

"You said you worked at Sweethearts, what, six months?" Shanahan shouted toward the kitchen.

"Eight months," he heard her say.

"You like it?"

"What's not to like?" she said, coming back in, handing him a bottle and a glass with Darth Vader on it. "This city's kinda quiet compared to some others I know. But it's probably about my speed."

"Why do you say that?"

"It's been a long time since anybody asked either one of us for our ID," she said without a trace of a smile. "You here to talk, you said?"

"Yeah," Shanahan said.

"It's okay by me. I'm a good listener." She sat back, looking at him, waiting.

"I'm thinking about buying Sweethearts," Shanahan said. "I really came here to find out more about the place before I sink some money into it."

"Is that right?" she asked.

"Yeah, you can look at the books and talk

to the owner, but the people who work there know what's really going on."

"A little slow on Tuesdays and Wednesdays. Mondays aren't bad. Thursdays are pretty busy. Friday's a lot better, and Saturday it's real crowded. When the soldiers at Fort Ben get paid, it's a bustling place." She stopped short, looked back at Shanahan like it was his move.

"That sounds pretty normal. You like the management?" Shanahan said uncomfortably. Things weren't going all that well. And he wasn't as smooth as he thought he'd be.

"Well, you've probably already talked with Mr. Grimes, then?"

"Sure," Shanahan said, "but like I said—"

Whatever he said must have pissed her off. She stood up, looking down at him. She looked like she was ready to spit on him.

"I don't know what your business is, but it isn't what you say it is." She pulled a can of mace from the cushion of the sofa. "So if you're a cop, you better show a badge and if you're not, you better haul ass outta here, now."

"Now, Sally—"

"Show or blow," she said, raising the little canister.

"I guess there's no Mr. Grimes, huh? A nice trick."

"And you're not, buddy. Out!" She raised the canister. "Now!" He was out the door.

Shanahan could hear the phone ringing in the darkness. He heard Maureen's voice. "Just a minute."

Something cold was being pressed against his face. "What?" Shanahan said when he discovered the cold something was the phone. "English, don't you understand that a man my age needs at least forty-five minutes sleep each night to stay alive?"

"Shanahan, listen. I went back to Sweethearts after you left. I promised Mai Lee I'd come back."

"When did you do that?" Shanahan asked.

"Well, when I went to the john I ran into her. . . ."

"She was in the john?" Shanahan was having trouble thinking.

"It's not important, that stuff . . . listen, the place was in an uproar. The cops came in and everybody thought it was a raid even though they came in real quiet. Well, it seems that the manager some guy named Dorfman or something, was blown up in his car. Wife too. Now get this, in front of the house of a guy named Marty Ray. He owns Sweethearts."

"What time?"

"About ten-thirty. What did you find out from the dancer?" English asked.

"That she used to dance with a snake."

"C'mon, Shanahan. Mai Lee told me there were rumors about Sweethearts being a coke connection. Coke as in cocaine. Ties in with Puckett. Mai Lee may be able to identify the photograph of Puckett. Maybe she knows who he hung around with."

"What kind of explosion?" Shanahan asked.

"A big one," English said, "blew in the big picture window."

"No, no, no, English. Pipe bomb, dynamite, grenade, what?"

"I'm sorry, I didn't think to ask. All right, I told you. Now what did you find out from your date?"

Someone was knocking on the door. "That she hated the snake and that she wasn't too fond of me. The snake died. And my bet is that she killed it. Now I gotta go." Shanahan hung up.

He went to the desk, picked up his .45 and went to the front door. He flipped on the light and peered into the eyes of the young police lieutenant. Shanahan stuffed the .45 under the pillow of the nearest chair.

"If it isn't Lieutenant Swann, with two N's."

"I'm sorry, Mr. Shanahan. I do have some questions. May I come in?"

"This is the worst part of the day, Billy," Leo said, barely making out Billy, a kind of gray shadow in front of a window, looking out into the early morning darkness. "Say something, Billy. Shit. It's too quiet, you know, too fucking quiet. Why in the hell you give 'em the gun, Billy?"

Billy laughed. It was the kind of laugh he always gave when he was making fun of something Leo said.

"It's not funny, goddammit."

"Seeing as though they had guns with bullets in 'em, kinda made sense to give up a gun that don't. Wouldn't you have figured it that way?"

"Then I wouldn't of pulled it out on 'em, then. Why'd you do that if you're smarter than I am?" Leo managed to put a little triumph in his question. "Laughing at me and stuff."

"If I didn't, they'd put gramps in here with us. He can't help us in here."

"You think he'll get us out?"

"I don't know." Both of them were quiet for a few minutes. "What are you thinking about?"

"About hearing what happened to this guy in the chair, about how it didn't kill him right away and they kept havin' to keep joltin' him, you know."

Billy could hear Leo breathing. "You all right?"

"Yeah," Leo said with a hoarse voice. "You see the sun yet?"

THIRTEEN

"What time did the kids get here?" Lieutenant Swann asked, sipping the coffee Maureen had brought him.

"Why?" Shanahan asked.

"Please," Swann said. "I'm tired. And if we're not careful, we're going to have a conversation. Conversations go on for hours.

So let me set the rules. One rule is that I get to ask the questions."

Shanahan liked him. Swann seemed like a decent guy. "I don't know," Shanahan said. "Maureen?"

"They were here when I got here, and I got here about eight-thirty," Maureen said. "They were waiting inside."

"They couldn't have," Shanahan said. "Where was Casey?"

"Your trusty guard dog was sitting at Leo's feet."

"My turn," Lieutenant Swann said. "Where were you, Mr. Shanahan?"

"No, it's my turn,' Shanahan said. "I have a rule too. My rule says you get a question, I get a question. What time did the bomb go off?"

"You know about that, do you?" Swann smiled. "The bomb went off at ten-thirty."

"Billy and Leo were already in your custody."

"Did you know about the fire at a boarded-up residence on Dearborn?"

"The kids' place?"

"Yep," Swann answered, staring back at Shanahan, trying to read him. "Happened at eight—rather, that's when fire department got there. Seems to me Dearborn is a pretty easy walk to your place."

"Surely you already checked the place for evidence. So what if it burned down?"

"Matter of fact, we didn't. We didn't know where they lived."

"How do you know they live there, then?"

"I'm doing all the answering, Mr. Shanahan. Makes me insecure, like I'm not a real police officer. Why do you think Billy and Leo burned down the house? Bloody clothes maybe?"

"Don't think so," Shanahan said.

"Why don't you think so?"

"I don't think there were any bloody clothes," Shanahan said. He wasn't going to say more and give the prosecution time to prepare a convenient theory.

"Maybe they were trying to destroy something else."

"What might that be?"

"Lisa Dennison. Her charred body was found on the second floor."

Shanahan closed his eyes. "Maybe . . ."

"It wasn't an accident, Mr. Shanahan. No falling asleep with a cigarette butt. Gas cans were found in the basement. Perhaps she could have put Billy and Leo at the scene of the Puckett stabbing."

"So your theory is that Billy and Leo killed Lisa, then went over and blew up Mr. Dorfman?"

"Dierdorf," Swann corrected him. "That's what you think I think, but I don't think so. I'm not even sure why you think they're connected. That's what interests me."

"Puckett was working on something that had to do with Sweethearts. Funny the manager of that establishment is blown up, don't you think?"

"Now that I see what track you're on . . . whoever took out Dierdorf used some pretty sophisticated explosives. And a clock. Now it's possible that the clock was put in his Lincoln much earlier, and that would keep your kids in the picture."

"Something they learned in the Cub Scouts, making bombs."

"I know," Swann said. "They could probably figure out a bomb or two, but none like this one. None of this takes them off the hook for Puckett or for the Dennison kid."

"So the prosecution will go after the Puckett conviction and have Lisa Dennison as insurance," Shanahan said.

"We don't convict. All we do is gather the

facts. A judge and jury puts them together. I'm not real eager to see these kids in the chair, Mr. Shanahan, and if there was ever a doubt they'd get it, it's gone now—they're in the web. Every time they move, they get more stuck."

"So the case is closed," Shanahan said. "They iced Puckett. They killed the girl. I think your job is more than getting a conviction. It's getting a just conviction. What about the Sweetheart connection?"

Swann stood, putting down his empty coffee cup. "I don't think there is a connection," Swann said. "Thanks for the coffee." He stopped at the door, turned. "Earlier this evening? Your .45? Didn't have the clip in. You owe me one. One more thing, while you're trying to save the kids, just be careful you don't get all tangled up with them. Have a nice day."

Shanahan tried to catch a meaning in the last comment. He couldn't. Swann spoke in flat, unemotional tones. But worse, Swann mentioning a web made Shanahan remember his dream. He couldn't be sure whether it was a spider's web or some strange abstraction of prison bars. Whatever, it was clear who was inside. It was Billy and Leo, nearly skeletal, eyes bulging, bellies bloated, gray flesh stuck to serrated strands of steel. Their mouths were open but there was no sound emanating.

Shanahan couldn't tell whether he was in there with them or outside looking in. Either way, he'd felt helpless. He felt helpless now.

It was only seven A.M. and Shanahan felt as if he'd already put in half a day's work, and there was still a whole day to go. He felt old this morning. He tossed the green tennis ball toward the fence in the backyard, and Casey, about as good a shortstop as a team could want, rounded off the grounder, catching it on the second bounce, bringing it back.

Shanahan believed he was getting old; but worse, he was getting sloppy. He should have checked out Billy and Leo's house long ago. He should have questioned Lisa Dennison. He should have found a way to get a good look at the driver of the red Caddy. Rafferty made a fool out of him on the license plate. He botched Sally what's-her-name from Sweethearts, and Lieutenant Swann got entirely too much information from him.

He tossed the ball again, sending Casey

out for a pop fly, and felt a twinge in his upper arm. Maybe he should just retire altogether. Hell, there weren't but a handful of baseball players in their forties. How many boxers or basketball players ever reached forty? And he had nearly seven decades on this earth. He shook his head.

The air was cool. Shanahan watched as the green ball descended, plopping into Casey's mouth. He took a deep breath, then laughed. "There's quite a few old-fart managers around in baseball, Casey," he said out loud. He reached down, picked up the tennis ball and flung it well over the high fence.

"Sorry, Case, just don't know my own strength."

"What are you doing?" Maureen asked. She brought him a sandwich and a cup of coffee, set it on the cluttered desk in the living room.

"What every good detective does in British mysteries. I'm listing all the suspects."

Maureen laughed. "But you only have one name."

"I know. Jennifer Bailey."

"Doesn't make for much of a gathering in the parlor, does it?" She took a bite of his sandwich. "By the way, it's your turn to fix dinner."

"I think I need to find out a little more about Sweethearts."

"Yeah, sure. Would you be so interested if the connection was with a hardware or a bakery?" She took a second bite out of his sandwich.

"Bakery maybe. Where I could eat my own sandwich."

"Here!" She thrust the sandwich in his face, laughing.

He took a bite. "Let's check out this Marty character."

"I'm invited?"

"Why not?" He wanted to keep her mind off her father. And short of a little duckpin bowling at Iria's, he couldn't think of a better way than to involve her in a bit of murder.

"Now what are you doing?"

"I'm putting two hundred-dollar bills into this envelope to Mr. and Mrs. Dunfy and a little note that says: 'Thanks for the tip, Mr. Dunfy, but as a professional investigator, I cannot accept it.' "

"What?"

"Just a little joke," Shanahan said. "I'd sure like to be there when Mrs. Dunfy opens this."

FOURTEEN

The house was in Meridian Hills. It was pretty much what they called modern in the 1950s—a flat-roofed ranch with a lot of angles. The blacktop driveway swung in from the street, then back out. The half circle it caused was heavily landscaped. The huge picture window was covered by sheets of plywood. On the front door was a little sticker: SEDMAN SECURITY, ELECTRONIC SURVEILLANCE.

Shanahan laughed to himself For $25 you got a sticker. That was it. And the sticker was supposed to scare off burglars. Marty Ray was the kind of guy who thought he could get by with something.

Marty couldn't take his eyes off Maureen. Shanahan realized that if it hadn't been for her, the guy might never have consented to talk, if that's what you called it.

"Hey look, what do I know?" Marty said, sitting on his plush white sofa. He wore a white V-neck sweater with nothing under it, a pair of tan shorts, and Top-Siders without socks—clothes that would have looked good on a young tennis player, say a Boris Becker, but not so good on a fiftyish, pudgy, balding man with a hairy chest. "I got a brother-in-law. Who knows what he's into, who he pissed off? Who says it's connected to Sweethearts? A gambling debt maybe."

"The police were investigating something connected to Sweethearts," Shanahan said.

"Police are always hanging out there. Any excuse to hang around naked women. Silvers would love to close down the place. Don't need no excuse except he don't want anybody having a good time. I say the guy's got sex problems, you know, like them TV preachers."

"The undercover cop who was shot was looking into your club," Shanahan said.

"Listen . . . fella. A place like Sweethearts . . . guys come in, the kinda guys you don't want hanging around, but they do. And they meet their friends there. And if some of 'em got a line on some coke, they make a deal while they're looking at the naked ladies. I can't stop that. You blame the McDonald's at thirty-eighth and Illinois for some youth-gang types that hang around there? You don't accuse the CEO of McD's of headin' up the gang. You want a drink?" he asked Maureen. "Sure you do. Orange juice, maybe a little something in it?"

"Plain's fine," Maureen said.

"Helen!" Marty bellowed. "So the cop hung out there, hoping to catch a little of the action, what am I supposed to do?"

"Don't yell, Marty," she said, appearing from the hall. Two large cats appeared at her feet, staring at the strangers in their house.

"This is Helen, my wife. Helen, this is Maureen, and what's your name again?"

"Shanahan."

Helen pursed her lips, nodded. Not a happy woman, Shanahan thought.

"Shanahan's a P.I. and he's thinking there's some connection between the cop that got shot and all this shit with your brother-in-law."

Helen's stare at Shanahan was interrupted by Marty asking her to get everybody some orange juice.

"Fuck off, Marty, I don't wait tables anymore," she said. "Nice to meet you." She spoke in the general direction of Shanahan and Maureen before disappearing into the hallway. Shanahan had the feeling she took a little mental snapshot of him before she left.

"She's upset about her sister."

"A rough way to go," Shanahan said. "Now, about a cop getting killed and the bomb that went off in your driveway . . ."

"C'mon, c'mon, c'mon." His words sounded like a burst from an automatic rifle. "It was a freakin' coincidence. A coupla kids offed the cop. You don't believe it. Happens all the time. Look at Vietnam. Little five-year-old Viet Cong took out bunkers with a grenade."

"You spend any time in the service? Korea maybe?"

"Naah."

"Your brother-in-law?"

"You gotta be kiddin'."

"You've got a beautiful place here, Marty," Maureen said.

"Yeah, lovely window, perfect view," he said, looking at the plywood.

"Your wife do this?" Maureen asked, looking out into the room.

"She's got some decorator friends."

"Could I get you to show me around?"

"Yeah, sure. Why the hell not? We'll start in the kitchen and I'll get you that orange juice, pretty woman." He looked at Shanahan, grinned. "You can come along too, if you promise not to get in the way."

A lot of brass, a lot of white. There was a Warhol Marilyn and a Warhol James Dean, a little color on the pale gray walls of the living room. Four bedrooms, one of which was occupied by Helen, who was diligently pedaling her ass off on a stationary bicycle. Not bad-looking, Shanahan thought, not bad-looking at all.

With money comes pretty blondes, swimming pools. He had already glanced through the windows to the garage—a Mercedes for him, a bright blue Mazda Miata convertible for her.

The room that led out to the pool would have made a horticulturalist proud. The overstuffed, tie-dyed furniture, rosewood bar, and marble floors would have purchased the interior designer a second home in Palm Springs.

"The art stuff is Helen's," Marty said. "The bar is mine, and I designed the pool."

"Sweethearts has been very good to you."

"True. That's where I met Helen, and the place has brought in some dough. But listen, this is years of work, Shanahan. I didn't have a daddy to pave the way. I worked my ass off to get that place going. Days without sleep, going in hock up to my jowls. It ain't drug money, kiddo. I've got mortgage and car payments."

Marty was working himself up. His face was red.

"So you and the others, Lieutenant Swann and them other creeps, can just take a hike."

"Just checking things out, that's all," Shanahan said. "I just don't think the kids could have killed a streetwise police detective. Puckett was a strong man, and he was stabbed in the chest."

"Calm down, Marry." It was Helen's voice. She was behind them. "Nicky's on the phone. She says two of the girls are talking about going to another club because of all the ruckus."

Marty looked at Maureen. "Sorry baby, everything's happening at once."

There were three messages on the answering machine. One was from English, wondering "what was up." The second was from Ms. Bailey, who pretty much asked the same question but took a few more words to do so. And the third was from Leo.

"I stood in line for a fuckin' hour and a half to use the phone and I get to talk to a goddam machine. I ain't with Billy no more. They put us in different places, so I don't know shit about what's goin' on."

"A lot of questions, Sherlock, and not much in the way of answers," Maureen said, rubbing Shanahan's shoulders. "You gonna add Marty to your vast list of prospects?"

Shanahan picked up the phone and dialed. "Lieutenant Swann, please." He looked up at Maureen. She looked tired, but not depressed. That was a good sign. "This is Shanahan. I just wondered. You know where Puckett's Caddy is? . . . Are you even looking for it? . . . Let me know where you find it . . . That's fine, Swann, and if I uncover something, I'll keep it to myself too."

Shanahan hung up the phone. Picked it up again. Dialed. "English, please."

"This is Tom English."

"Shanahan."

"What's up?"

"That's what I want to know. You're the reporter."

"Sometimes I'm a food critic."

"What's that supposed to mean?"

"It means I'm officially off the story. Things are crazier than hell. Sarah's back. Connell stormed out. The art director said that Sarah bought the magazine. Now she wants to drop the story and has me checking out some new Northside restaurant. It's like she's on some power trip. Fact is, I don't get it. Connell is supposed to be worth millions. How could she buy it from him, especially if he didn't want to sell?"

"So are you dropping the story?"

"Paul said Connell inherited the money and that he's gone through it all, that he's as dumb as a box of rocks."

"Are you dropping the story?"

". . . Uh, no," English said, as if just now making up his mind.

"Good."

"But I can't do it on company time."

"Yeah, well never mind. It's okay." Shanahan tapped his pencil on the desk. He felt like an amateur. He and Maureen visiting Marty and getting nowhere. Sophisticated plastic bombs. A kid getting burned to death in an abandoned house. An ambitious prosecutor and an entire police force dedicated to send the kids away for life, or death, for that matter. And he was depending on a boy reporter. Jesus. It was like a Hardy Boys.

"Wait a minute." English's voice was angry. "All I said was I can't do it on company time. What do you want? Want me to find the Cadillac?"

"Yeah, that'll do for starters." Shanahan shook his head and smiled. He hung up the phone, looked at Maureen. "What else have I got to do?"

He picked up the phone again, dialed.

"How 'bout dinner?" Maureen asked. "Remember, your turn to cook."

"Maybe Delaney's got some stew on."

"Tom English," he said into the phone.

"It doesn't count if we go out," Maureen said. "Didn't you already talk to him?"

"English?"

"Didn't I just talk to you?"

"The girl, Lisa what's-her-name . . ."

"The girl who was burned? Lisa Dennison."

"Nobody knew about her."

"What do you mean?"

"I mean you knew about her from me. Leo's sister. Me. The cops, but only afterward. Did you talk to anybody?"

"No. I haven't even written it down in the story yet. I made some rough notes. That was all."

"Where?"
"On the computer."
"Who can get in your computer?"
"Anybody with half a brain."
"Make a list for me."
"What difference does it make?"
"The killer knew about Lisa Dennison. That means it was somebody who knew Leo and Billy pretty well, or found out about it later and killed the kid because she knew something or to make sure Leo and Billy would fry."
"Oh." English was quiet. "Nobody at the magazine would be involved in this."
"English, you told me your boss took a special interest in this case, right?"
"Yeah. Connell."
"Then your, what . . . editor took you off it after some shenanigans about who owns the magazine."
"Yeah."
"No, you're right. It doesn't make sense. Good-bye."
Maureen put her hand on Shanahan's shoulder. "Jennifer Bailey knew about Lisa Dennison. You said that Billy and Leo told you at the jail. Wasn't counsel there?"
Shanahan sat back in his chair. "Yeah," he said, drawing out the word. He shook

his head. "Jennifer Bailey could be capable of an act of murder out of jealousy. Passion gives you strength. She could have killed Puckett. But killing a kid in cold blood?"

They sat in the booth at Delaney's bar. Delaney brought Shanahan and Maureen a plate of stew just as Harry walked in, sliding in beside Maureen.

"Hi, gorgeous," Harry said to Maureen. She liked Harry, and even if she hadn't, she wouldn't have broken up the only friendship Shanahan seemed to have.

"Hi, handsome, looking for a good time?" Maureen replied.

"By Jesus, I think I've found it—that is, if Shanahan over there can take a hint."

Shanahan looked up at the oversized screen in the corner of the bar. Football highlights. The quarterback had his arm cocked, ready to send the football way downfield. Then some bruiser broke through the line and the quarterback made one last futile look downfield and crouched over, ready to take the hit. Shanahan's eyes glazed over. He always hated it when football season started. They allowed it to drown out the best part of the baseball season. Pretty soon they'd be playing football year 'round.

"He isn't listening, Harry." Maureen said, putting her hand on his forearm. "We could sneak out for a few hours and he'd never know we were gone.

"Hairy, I need to see the coroner's report on Puckett."

"The cop?"

"The very one."

"I'm about to steal your girl, Deets."

"Can you do it?"

"One way or another. Why? The news said it was a stab wound, straight to the heart. That'll do the job. And why you so interested? They got them little punks with the goods. You involved in this thing, Deets?"

"The kids didn't do it."

"Who are you working for?"

"Me."

"You suddenly become Spencer Tracy in *Boys' Town?*" Harry asked.

"The kids always wear the same clothes, Harry. They wore the same clothes at the time of the murder, and afterward and there was no blood on them. When the knife hit the heart, it shot blood out all over the room like a gusher."

"All right. But why do you need the coroner's report?"

"To see if there was a blow to the head or something first. Or drugs that would put him out."

"Why?" Maureen asked, suddenly interested.

"The kids told me the guy was lying on his back. No other cuts, clothing intact, and the blade stuck in the heart." In Shanahan's mind he could see a rerun of the quarterback getting his body in a position to take the hit. "If what they say is true, then there were no signs of a struggle."

"So maybe he knew the killer?" Maureen asked, between bites of her stew.

"Wait a minute, Deets," Harry said, "even if he knew the killer, he'd try to defend himself if he saw a knife coming at him. He was stabbed straight on in the front."

"That's pretty much how I see it."

"Maybe he thought it was a joke," Maureen said.

"Maybe he was blindfolded or something," Harry added.

"Maybe," Maureen said, "he thought the person was bluffing and stood there like some he-man."

"And who would he do that for? Be macho?"

"A woman," Maureen said.

"Or a couple of scrawny kids," Harry said.

At home, Shanahan let Casey out the back. He heard the familiar snorting that meant Casey had found something. A possum probably. Casey had various sounds, and after five years with the dog, Shanahan had come to understand what they meant. He had a bark for cats, who he would merely terrorize if he got the chance. He had one bark for someone a little too near the house and another for a legitimate threat.

The snorting meant he'd uncovered a scent, but not the invader. It continued, and while Maureen undressed in the bedroom, Shanahan called Casey in, took his flashlight out in the back. He heard scratching sounds on the trunk of the giant maple tree. He flashed the light up and caught what he thought was a cat, much like Einstein—a ringed tail—lodging himself in the crook between branches. It was a young racoon. It stared back. Shanahan was afraid that Casey would kill the young creature, and he thought for a moment of getting his ladder and taking it out of the yard.

The racoon looked frightened, no more dangerous than Shanahan's cat. But Shanahan knew better. The little creature was dangerous, especially because he was frightened. Immediately, Shanahan thought of Billy and Leo.

He kept Casey inside the rest of the night, and hoped that the racoon would get tired of the tree and wander off somewhere. It had a wild scent. Casey would kill it, as sure as the State of Indiana would kill Billy and Leo, the government thinking they had done right, what they were elected to do. And there it was. It was the way the world was, wasn't it?

And there she was. Maureen was in bed. He could see from the hall, the hall light sending into the dark room a broad stripe of light that showed her nude body on the white sheets.

Shanahan thought of her father on his death bed a hundred miles south. He thought of a frightened Billy and Leo now separated and stranded, unprepared, at the mercy of bigger, tougher men in the Marion County jail. He thought of the poor little girl Lisa, burned in the house, and Leo's sister at the factory.

"Hey, Deets! Shanahan!" Maureen called to him as he stood momentarily frozen in the hall. "You want to talk about it?"

"No," Shanahan said.

"You want to make love?"

Shanahan came into the room, undressed. He crawled in beside her and felt her hands travel familiar routes, and he laughed to himself about how fickle the mind was, how quickly it forgot tragedies and injustices.

"Harry told me about that little dancer you were madly in love with in Paris," Maureen said, propping her pillow against the headboard. In the darkness, Shanahan couldn't see the slight smile on her face.

"Harry has a big mouth."

"Was she pretty?"

"Yes," Shanahan said.

"Did you have a cigarette afterward?"

"Yes."

"Was she beautiful?"

"You already asked that question."

"No," Maureen said. "I asked if she was pretty. Now I'm asking if she was beautiful?"

"Yes."

"You remember. Must have been thirty years ago."

"More than forty," Shanahan said. "You are younger than she is now, if she's still alive."

"Am I prettier now than she was then, this Follies' girl?"

"She was a ballerina."

"That was a two-part question. Am I prettier now than she was then?"

"No."

She pinched his arm—hard—then kissed him. "Do you always have to tell the truth? Do you have a picture of her?"

"No. Listen, Harry likes to live in the past. I don't."

"I like Harry."

"I didn't say you didn't like Harry."

"He has many interests."

"Harry likes the Chicago Cubs, euchre, beer, and women. In that order."

"What's *your* list like, Shanahan?"

He tried to think of something other than what he was thinking about.

"Right now it's two fucking little kids sitting in a goddam stinkhole with a bunch of animals who—"

"I'm sorry," Maureen said. She ran her

hand over Shanahan's chest. "I forget . . ." She didn't complete the sentence. She was going to say "I forget how much you care." But that was not the kind of thing to say to Shanahan. She wanted to ask him if he ever cried, if he loved her as much as she loved him.

FIFTEEN

Shanahan had seen fine houses before. In the course of his duties in Europe, he'd seen some of the grandest in the world. But these many years later, his modest income as a P.I. and the circles in which he traveled had not prepared him for the Connell estate.

Surprisingly, after identifying himself as Dietrich Shanahan at the two-way speaker at the gate, a soft melodious voice told him to travel the drive which would lead him to the main house and he would be given directions there.

Directions to where? he wondered. Seeing the dented hood of his '72 Chevy Malibu float on the flawless, curving blacktop drive made Shanahan feel like a sharecropper.

Suddenly, he could see the house. Shanahan was taken with it. He could have been back in France. The home was immense, two-story brick and stone, each section having its own high slate roof. The drive circled a center garden. Waiting at the entrance was an attractive black woman.

"I thought you'd have a truck," she said as he pulled up beside her.

"Do I look like a truck driver?" Shanahan replied, knowing full well strangers never knew when he was kidding. He tried to smile, but as usual it came out a grimace.

"I don't know how you're going to do it unless you're a magician," she said. "Back up, take the gravel road to the east of the house. You'll go down a little hill, and once you're down there, you'll see the shed."

"Is Mr. Connell in?"

"He isn't in. It's Mrs. Connell you want. I told Mr. Fisher that, and she's down in the shed."

Shanahan followed directions. But he didn't see any "shed." What was before him was a beautiful brick building many times smaller than the main house, but built in the same style and with the same care. It looked like a stable perhaps. Behind it was a huge pond surrounded by long grasses.

And at that instant three ducks flew off from its calm water.

"Mrs. Connell," Shanahan said, addressing a very beautiful woman. She was a slim, fit woman in her fifties. Her hair hung straight with strands of gray and gold and brown. Her face was well-tanned and she wore a blue workshirt and a pair of men's jeans.

"You're early," she said, her green eyes quickly sizing him up. Her face was lined, but Shanahan could tell the difference between lines of age and worry and lines caused by the wind and sun. Unlike Helen Ray, Mrs. Connell looked like a person who couldn't bear to lie idly under the rays for the cosmetic look. She struck him as active and energetic.

She sat behind a potter's wheel, her hands covered in gray-brown liquid. A huge, five-foot pot was on the wheel, at one side. Mrs. Connell's right foot was poised over the pedal. She seemed disappointed.

"Are you sure you can handle these?" she asked, nodding toward a dozen or so more pots of equal size lined against the wall behind him.

He turned and looked.

"I'll help," she said, getting up. "I moved

them here, so surely I can help you get them into your truck. You've brought the packing materials I requested?"

"You sail, Mrs. Connell?"

"Yes. How did you know?"

"Lucky guess. Judging by the depth of your tan, it looks like you enjoy the outside. I'm afraid I've somehow misrepresented myself. I didn't mean to."

"What are you talking about?"

"I came to talk with your husband."

"My husband is rarely here at this hour. What is it you wanted with him?"

"Conversation."

She laughed heartily. "I'm afraid I can be of no help to you there. He and I haven't had a conversation in seven years."

She got up, went to the side and moved one of the pots, rolling it, then lifting it up over a high piece of lumber Shanahan guessed to have been part of a horse's stall.

"Can I help?"

"No. I'm used to it. What kind of conversation? Perhaps I can direct you to the appropriate secretary."

"It's about the death of a policeman. I'm a private investigator."

She set the pot up next to the others, stood, looked him straight in the eye.

"What has my husband to do with a policeman's death?"

"Probably nothing at all," Shanahan said.

Mrs. Connell gave a half grin. "Was it something Gothic and horrible?"

"You haven't read about it?"

"No. I don't take the papers." She smiled. "I don't watch television. I make pots, go sailing, and read books about aging women with handsome young men. Have you ever read Colette?"

It was Shanahan's turn to laugh. "No, I haven't."

"I didn't think you had, Mister . . ."

"Shanahan. Dietrich Shanahan."

"Mr. Shanahan, then. It's just that I thought I liked you, but I had to make sure you had a sense of humor. Men with no sense of humor kill. I mean 'kill' in the sense of spirit. You have no idea what it's like to live with a man who never laughs."

"My wife never laughed." He didn't know what made him say this to a perfect stranger, or why in fact did he now think about the woman who left him a couple of decades ago. "Why has Mr. Connell taken such a sudden interest in the *Metro Monthly?*"

"Has he? It's probably a phase. He fancies himself as different people sometimes. When things go badly in one part of his life, he pretends that isn't his life. Besides, he likes to dabble. He's very much a dabbler. He likes to spend his father's money, which he does rather well.

"I always thought that family businesses ought to skip a generation. It was his father's money. Even accounting for inflation, my husband is worth less than he was when his father died. Sons of successful businessmen rarely are . . . successful."

"I don't know much about those things, Mrs. Connell."

"My name is Lenora. It wasn't, but I changed it to be fashionable, and now that I don't give a damn about fashion, I'm stuck with the pretense. I guess I deserve it. At any rate, in the Connell family intelligence seemed to have skipped two generations. I'm afraid young Jimmy isn't too bright either. He's picked his father as a role model. But sons get the money and daughters get the brains."

"You've been very helpful," Shanahan said. He liked her. He wouldn't attempt a diplomatic good-bye with most people.

"No, of course I haven't been helpful and

you don't lie very well at all. I don't know anything about the policeman's death. And the only thing I know about my husband these days is that he's dyeing his hair, which means he's having another affair. And bless her, she's finally gotten him to buy a decent pair of shoes."

"Well . . ."

"I know," she said. "You didn't come here to listen to stories better left for the hairdresser. And I'm keeping you too long. I'm sure that if there's any mystery connected to Jim's life, it is merely a pretty face."

"Why did you marry him, Mrs. Connell?"

"He was young, handsome, in uniform, and had a great deal of money."

"Thanks," Shanahan said.

"Not true. Well yes, it was true. But I didn't need the money. I have more than he does. What I wanted was the house. I wanted this house ever since I was a child and played with Jim down by the pond. He was seven and I was six. I knew it then. I also knew that when his father died, because Jim was the son, we would have it. I usually get what I want, Mr. Shanahan. Unfortunately, we also get what we deserve." There was more than a little touch of irony in her voice. "Do you sail?"

"No." Shanahan smiled.

"That's too bad," she said, in a way that Shanahan gladly interpreted as a flirtation.

"You're a very attractive woman, Mrs. Connell."

"In the right light," she said.

Shanahan woke up a little after nine. Beside him was Maureen's imprint in the sheets. She was outside, in the backyard, inspecting the lily bed, occasionally stooping down and pulling up some invading weed. The blooms were gone, disappeared in late August, maybe September. But Maureen had read up on growing lilies and she knew the importance of their having as much fall sun as possible to bloom well next June. She also had a bag of phosphate she sprinkled on the ground around the lilies, something she learned from reading.

Maureen had on her high-waisted khaki shorts and short-sleeve white shirt. The sun brought out the subtle red highlights in her long hair. Shanahan regretted not telling her she was prettier than the French ballerina.

He sat down at his desk in the living

room, glad the view afforded him glimpses of Maureen. He loved it when he could watch her without her knowing. If she knew, she'd put on a little show.

First he called English and told him to drop the search for the red Caddy. He should have known better than ask the kid to do it. English was a reporter, but Harry would know how to track it down faster. English was relieved. Shanahan asked him to find out what he could about the Sarah Mundy–James Connell deal with the magazine.

"Why are you so interested in that?" English asked.

"I'm not sure," Shanahan said, and he wasn't. However, there was something strange about the sudden interest and subsequent sudden lack of interest in the story of Billy and Leo.

He dialed Harry's number. Harry's wife said he had just left, that he was going to Delaney's. It was too early for drinking, even for Harry, and besides, Delaney didn't open until eleven. Harry's wife said they had some deal going.

Shanahan felt a rush of energy. His mind was clicking for a change. He looked out the window at Maureen, hunched down in the lilies, and thought maybe it was because of last night and sleeping until he was ready to wake up. God, he hoped she'd never leave him. He wondered if the inevitable death of her father—who was a few years younger than he—would somehow make a difference. Would she regret taking up with a man she'd outlive by a few decades?

He put it out of his mind and called Jennifer Bailey. She'd left instructions not to be interrupted. She was in a meeting, the slightly curt voice of her male secretary told him.

"Two minutes, Steve," Shanahan told him, surprised and happy that he could remember the name. Though he'd never admit it, Shanahan worried about senility and he kept a mental scorecard on memory lapses.

"I didn't want to talk to you, Mr. Shanahan," Jennifer Bailey said.

"You have bad news."

"They're rushing the trial."

"Ask for delays, stays, or whatever in the hell you attorneys do to keep cases in the court for twenty years."

"I tried," Jennifer Bailey said. "They're not granting. I know what you're thinking."

"What's that?"

"That a rush to judgment is precisely what I want. Isn't that right?"

"Yes, I thought about that."

"You still don't believe me, do you, Shanahan?"

He didn't. The idea that Puckett would have allowed someone to stab him in the chest because he thought the killer was bluffing fit in real nice with Jennifer Bailey. Wronged woman. Jealousy. Passion.

"I believe," Shanahan said, "a woman killed him." He didn't elaborate.

"Maybe it was the woman he was seeing, Mr. Shanahan. Maybe he told her about me. He did send me flowers."

"Maybe." She was cool, he thought. So quick with the answers. Too cool.

When he hung up, he'd already decided what he would do. He'd stop by Delaney's and talk with Harry, and then he'd be out at the factory and catch Leo's sister, Edie, at lunch break.

"You want a drink now?" Maureen said when Shanahan walked out in the yard. There was no accusation, just surprise in her voice. She never laid a guilt trip on him for anything. She was so beautiful. It was a fine fall morning, just that faint, hardly recognizable chill from the north in an otherwise warm, sunny day.

"I need to talk with Harry. I'll be gone most of the day."

"I'll be fine. I've got my real estate books all stacked up in the order I'm supposed to read them. And it's my turn to fix dinner." She made a disgusted face. She hated cooking.

"We'll go out."

"Not stew at Delaney's."

"No. We'll go somewhere else, Ambrosia's in Broad Ripple or maybe Laughner's Cafeteria." There was little she liked more than food, and she loved the idea that it was all spread out for her to choose from. What with bingeing Häagen-Dazs Swiss vanilla almond and Pepperidge Farm cookies, it's a wonder she wasn't a blimp.

"Thanks," she said. "I got a call this morning. My sister." Shanahan tried to read her face, but she gave no clue. "Dad died last night." Still nothing. He'd known a few poker players who could do that—not register anything.

"Are you going down?" Shanahan hated these moments. Normal people could show sympathy, knew what to say. He was also angry that he wasn't thinking of her so much as himself. He didn't want her to go. He imagined weeks settling the estate. He didn't want her withdrawing again, getting distant. What a selfish ass he was.

"No." She looked away, then stooped down to pull at a two-inch weed. "I talked with Barbara and she's going to take care of everything. I'll go down the day of the funeral. Drive down and drive back."

"Are you doing this for me?" Shanahan asked.

She stood up. "No. I'm doing it for me. Like you said last night about not living in the past. Dad and I had our chance to settle some things. We didn't. We can't now. I'd rather be here with you than with some dead . . ." She kissed him lightly on the cheek, didn't finish her sentence. "Tell Harry I said hi."

On the drive over, Shanahan couldn't help but marvel at Maureen. Her humor, energy. In the eight months he'd known her, there had been only this one period where darkness descended, this period of grief for her father.

She would share her humor. She would share her energy, lifting his spirits, making him feel human after decades of withdrawal, allowing him to be himself and loving him for it. But she would not share her grief. She took it inside her, dealt with it and came out stronger. He had never met anyone like her—a lover and friend.

"Half the people who come in here," Shanahan said to Harry, who huddled with Delaney in one of the booths that lined the wall, "come here for Delaney's stew. What are you going to do about that?"

"I told him," Delaney said, a sheepish or maybe guilty look on his face. "I told him, showed him the books. The costs go up, the sales go down."

"Here are the facts," Harry said. "Delaney wants to go fishing in Fort Myers the rest of his life, and he's gonna sell the bar whether he sells it to me or some dufus. I don't want the bar to get in the wrong hands. I'll keep it like it is."

"What do you know about running a bar?" Shanahan asked, slipping in the booth beside Delaney.

"I practically grew up in one. Wisconsin. All they got in Wisconsin is bars and churches. That's the way God intended it. You go to the bar six days a week and you go to church on the seventh. Ain't that the way it is, Delaney?" Delaney shrugged. "I spend half my wakin' hours in bars and I'm in this one almost as much as Delaney is. I know all the regulars."

"What's left of 'em," Delaney said. "What ain't died or gone to the home."

"Harry—" Shanahan began, not knowing what he was going to say, but it didn't make any difference because Harry was stubborn and he was interrupted anyway.

"You just want me at your beck and call, Deets."

"I told him, Shanahan, honest to God. The bar's got to change, keep up with the times."

"Christ be Jesus, Delaney, I ain't puttin' up with no goddam ferns and brunches and shit like that."

"This is the Eastside, Harry. Ain't nobody gonna be puttin' in ferns. Face it. Needs to be a rock 'n' roll joint or a stripper bar or something. I can't do that. Neither can you," Delaney said. "Why in the hell do you think I'm tryin' to sell the place?"

"You stubborn Irishmen are all alike," Harry said, switching his gaze from Delaney to Shanahan, then back to Delaney, who just kept shaking his head. "You're gonna sell the friggin' bar. Here's somebody settin' right here before you who's got the money you're asking for the place and practically begging on his hands and knees and you're waffling around like a kite on a short string."

Delaney looked at Shanahan. He was nervous. He looked back at Harry, then back at Shanahan. "What the hell am I supposed to do? My friend wants me to help him go bankrupt."

"Sell it," Shanahan said. "What'd you find out from the coroner, Harry?"

"Short and sweet. The report," he said, pulling some badly crumpled papers from his hip pocket and handing them to Shanahan, "says stab wound. Read it all you want. Nothing about no other damages, chemical or physical. Now that you're here, you can witness the transaction."

"Excuse me," Delaney said, and Shanahan got up to let him out of the booth.

"Delaney's got fifty cases of Miller High Life beer in the long-necked bottles in the basement," Harry said when Delaney was out of earshot.

"So?"

"Deets, he got 'em so you'd never run out. I mean, you call me funny and set in my ways. You're so goddam particular about them clear glass tall bottles he ordered special 'cause he thought the company might discontinue them. Won't let nobody else have one. Cause he's one helluva guy."

"Is that why you're buying the bar, because he's one helluva guy?"

"You owe me fifty bucks, Mr. Dietrich Shanahan smartass detective."

"How'd you get it from them?"

"Trade secret," Harry said smugly. "You pay fifty bucks for the goods and you pay a fortune extra if you want to know the technique." He raised his eyebrows a few times and smiled. "Fifty bucks, I figure, for the report."

"Put it on my tab," Shanahan said.

"Tab, you say? Now, just who says I'm gonna let you run a tab. What kind of businessman do you think I am?"

"You can't afford to lose any regulars. I figure I'm good for maybe a hundred beers a month."

"Not since you started hanging out with Maureen, you're not. Besides, you sittin' around here all stern-faced, never laughing at my jokes and not talking to the clientele, you scare the customers off."

"Can you track down a red Caddy for

me? Nineteen eighty-eight or -nine, white top, two doors, license plate 'Flat one-two.' "

"Maybe."

"Belonged to Puckett. It's missing."

"I'm supposed to drive around the city and check half a million garages?"

"I don't know. You're the one with the technique. You might narrow the garages down to Jennifer Bailey's, property owned by Marty what's-his-name who owns Sweethearts, and James Connell."

"Connell the big shot?"

"One and the same. He could own some obscure places around town big enough and isolated enough to stash a car without anyone knowing. So could Marty. Oh, and check out Sarah Mundy. She works at the *Metro Monthly.*"

"Well, I do have a bar to run, Deets. I'm a man of responsibility."

"Baseball season is over, Harry, and besides, it'll take a while before you can get the liquor license. They check out people like you."

"Fuck you, you Irish kraut," Harry said.

"Maureen says hi."

"Don't let her slip through your fingers

like you did that pretty little Frenchy in Paris."

"Yeah."

"Maybe Maureen could wait tables. She'd bring in the business. Some new blood."

"I'll mention it."

"No you won't, Deets. And if I were you, I wouldn't either."

SIXTEEN

After witnessing Harry's intent letter to buy Delaney's for a sum Shanahan found difficult to believe his old friend had, he headed out to Upshank Manufacturing to talk with Leo's sister, Edie. He wasn't quite sure why. He did something else on the way, something he also did out of some vague instinct. He drove up through Meridian Hills toward Marty and Helen's.

Helen, her blond hair tied back, sitting in her little blue Miata, was pulling out of the driveway as he pulled up. She slowed, then stopped where the drive met the street. He got out of the car and went over to her.

"Can I help you?" she said, her voice not particularly friendly.

"I met you—"

"Yes, I know. You're a private investigator. Something I can help you with? I'm rather in a hurry."

The "rather" sounded a little phony, and Shanahan could make out an airline ticket stuck between the pages of *Elle* magazine. U.S. Air. If she had luggage, it was in the trunk.

"I thought I'd ask Marty a few more questions."

"Well," she said icily, "Marty isn't here." She stepped on the accelerator.

Shanahan would have to be late for lunch with Edie. He'd catch her at afternoon break. He didn't attempt to tail the little blue convertible, but took his own route to the airport. He knew the airline, so he knew which terminal. And Indianapolis International wasn't all that big.

He found her in the short-term parking garage. And she got nothing from the trunk. Left her car, top down. He picked her up again midway down the U.S. Air wing, standing impatiently, carrying only a purse. It was a short trip, obviously. If it had been to Chicago or New York, he might be satisfied with the idea she was going for a little shopping spree. But Detroit?

Shanahan saw no need to hang around. He walked back to the airport to the automatic cash machine and took out a twenty. If he didn't, he wouldn't be able to get out of the parking garage. He thought about Detroit, about organized crime, about the plastic bomb that blew up her sister and brother-in-law.

Though he knew little about syndicates in Indianapolis, he had heard that the city was not particularly organized. They were around—Dayton, Toledo, maybe. The Chicago mob had northwestern Indiana—Gary, Hammond, East Chicago, South Bend. And Detroit was moving into Fort Wayne in the northeast. But no heavy-hitters here. At least he didn't think there were.

Marty could have come from a casting expert. He looked like the small-time gangster type, and Helen wasn't exactly miscast as the blond girlfriend. But what was the girlfriend doing in Detroit? A pickup? Cocaine? She could bring a bundle back in a shopping bag.

"Neither of them smoke," Edie said, sitting at the picnic-type table in the stark room where the workers took their breaks. "At least nothin' you could take into a jail." She was drinking a Diet Coke and munching on a Snickers bar. "The little shits," she said.

Shanahan found he did have little to say and not much to ask when he finally heard the buzzer for the afternoon break. He had wanted to know if there was anything he could take to Billy and Leo.

"Do they read?"

"Read? Billy and Leo?" She made a sad little laugh. "Billy reads comic books, if you call that readin'."

"What kind?" Shanahan said quickly, surprised he really wanted to know.

"I don't know what kind. Comic books. But not the funny kind. I remember seeing something with an X on the front and I asked him if that meant X-rated and he said sort of. Only I looked at them and they didn't look like they had sex in them or anything."

"Where are their parents, Edie?"

"Ain't gonna come." She shook her head, seemed like she was ready to cry. Then it looked like she was going to explain, but shook her head again, raised hands that said there was nothing she or anybody could do about it.

He really only had one more question he wanted to ask her. It seemed cruel because he was pretty sure he knew the answer and it wouldn't change anything.

"Are you still seeing Lieutenant Rafferty?"

She didn't say anything, just shook her head no and peeled back the paper on her Snickers bar. She took a bite, more to keep from crying than because she wanted more candy. But all of a sudden it seemed too hard to chew.

"Thanks," he said. She stared off.

"You're a real sweet guy, Rafferty," Shanahan said to himself as he walked back out to the lot. "So are you, Shanahan," he reminded himself.

Shanahan called Maureen, asked if she'd look up Comics in the Yellow Pages. She found a place in Broad Ripple, and the guy in the comic shop knew exactly what kind of comic had an X in the title. It was *X-Men,* and the man in the shop full of comics old and new had just gotten the new issue that morning. Shanahan bought it and a few others the guy said were in the same vein.

He stopped in at Jennifer Bailey's and, as had become his recent habit, called her out of a meeting to give her the comic books to give to Billy.

She looked at him as if he were insane, but took them. She said the best she could do was keep them from the death penalty, since "we"—and she definitely included Shanahan in the pronoun—"were unable to turn up anything that could shake the case."

Shanahan explained to her about the clothing, how the blood would have splattered them and how an eye witness had seen the kids in the same clothes just before and after the murder. She listened.

When he was done, she took off her glasses, rubbed her eyes. She looked as if she might cry. That would be two out of three, he thought. Jennifer Bailey and Edie. Helen wasn't the type, he thought.

"It's not that I don't believe you. I do. And yes, this is something we could bring up. But this isn't *Perry Mason* or *Matlock*. Courts just don't work that way. The jury will find it all very interesting, but it won't do it. Instead of being this dramatic event you're picturing, Mr. Shanahan, or cause someone to break down and confess, the prosecution will make it all seem convoluted and confusing. In the end, the boys had the money, blood on the shoes, fingerprints all over the place. All this is witness to their presence at the scene. This coupled with their less than exemplary record will mean conviction. I'm sorry. That's not the way I want it to be, but someone has to remain sane and see that this is the way it is."

"Delay the proceedings, so we can find the car?"

"What car?"

"The red Cadillac, Ms. Bailey."

She looked funny. "His?"

"Yes. It was parked near my house when the police came to arrest Billy and Leo. And later, the same car was at Sweethearts."

"This is all very interesting. But you don't understand the law. A stolen car is, at best, irrelevant to this case. I'm sorry."

"Delay the trial, Ms. Bailey, or I will."

"*You* will?"

"As a friend of the court, I'll explain that the defense attorney has a conflict of interest."

"If I deny it, Mr. Shanahan, which I will,

they will think you're just a wee bit loony." She looked more amused than frightened.

"Why aren't you looking out for the kids' interests?"

"I am. The city's in a hanging mood, Mr. Shanahan. And like it or not, given the facts in this case—a prosecutor who will use the idea of a cop killer, gang-killing, and the fact that the victim was black, therefore a racist killing—a black female attorney has the best chance of keeping them alive. You'll have to trust me. Take the long-shot odds, get a delay on the remote chance you will find something that will really clear them, really clear them from both the killing of the cop and of the girlfriend, on which they are about to be charged as a matter of insurance; and if you fail, they will die."

So strange, Shanahan thought. Just when he thought he had her cornered, she came out even stronger. He always seemed to come out the worst.

He wondered if she were strong enough to plunge a bayonet in Puckett's chest. There were documented cases where women lifted automobiles off their children. Adrenaline was a mighty thing, he thought.

"Are you willing to send me packing on a long shot? If you are, remember you are gambling with their lives."

"Make sure Billy gets the comics," he said, heading toward the door.

"I will, Mr. Shanahan."

He turned back. "What happened to the woman who swore she knew those kids didn't do it?"

"She's still here. She's also an attorney who's practiced law for twelve years, and she knows that justice, at best, is only approximate."

SEVENTEEN

Shanahan was hungry. But he decided to swing by the long, low ranch in Meridian Hills that belonged to Marty and Helen Ray. He thought with Helen gone and Marty probably at the club, he could at least check out the house for electronic surveillance, find out if there was a way inside, to learn more about the unhappy couple.

Marty's Mercedes was in the drive. Shanahan thought for a moment, then pulled behind it. The green '72 Chevy Malibu, which at 150,000 miles had lived longer than GM intended, didn't belong in this neighborhood. He'd bought it used in '78 because it was plain enough for his kind of work. Now, he realized, it was so old it stood out.

Marty answered the door and was obviously disturbed at the interruption.

What he said when Shanahan asked him what he'd heard from the police about the explosion that killed his in-laws was: "Look, I'm not too fond of guys who put their noses up other people's butts and start sniffin' around. Now, I was nice to you because you were with a babe young enough to be your daughter."

"How's your wife, Marty?" Shanahan asked pointedly.

"Yeah, well, I can afford pretty young things," Marty said, appraising the private detective.

"I get by on my looks," Shanahan said.

Marty laughed. He softened. "No offense, guy. But I come home between the lunch crowd and the dinner crowd and I like to take a nap, sit out by the pool and stare at the drain, you know. I got a long night ahead of me, what with my manager gettin' blown to smithereens, so I'd just as soon not stand out here and beat my gums."

Shanahan wanted inside, just to look around, maybe get him to tell him why his wife was doing a day trip to Detroit.

"You suppose I could use your phone? Two minutes, then out of your life."

"Okay, handsome," Marty said, stepping aside. "Use the one in the breakfast room, just off the kitchen."

"Where's the wife?" Shanahan asked, moving toward the phone.

"How the fuck do I know?" Marty yelled.

Shanahan wondered if he should ask about Detroit, and if so, how. Instead of dialing, he pushed the redial button and waited. On the third ring a man's voice said: "Howard Cross—private investigation."

Shanahan pressed the button and got the dial tone, looked around. No papers on the table or the kitchen, nothing pinned up on the wall or stuck on the fridge. They kept the place spotless. Shanahan wondered how anybody could live like that. It looked like a show home. Besides being too sterile to live in, it yielded very little about who the residents were.

He dialed home. Maureen answered.

"I'm hungry," Shanahan said.

“I’m horny,” Maureen said.

Shanahan felt himself blush. She liked doing that to him.

“Thanks for the information,” Shanahan said. “Don’t answer the door, it might be the paper boy.”

“Don’t worry, he’s not that good in bed.”

Shanahan hung up. “You mind if I use your bathroom?” Shanahan said, coming into the room and finding Marty standing there, hands on his hips.

“Hey! You want to fix yourself a bite to eat, go for a swim, take a nap?”

“C’mon, what’s another two minutes?”

“Down the hall. You gotta fuckin’ hold up the lid with your knee ’cause Helen puts those fluffy, crappy covers on it. And don’t piss on it. She’ll think I did it.”

He passed Helen’s exercise room. Noticed that besides a stationary bicycle, she had a Nautilus machine. The bathroom yielded nothing unusual. Basic stuff in the medicine cabinet. He figured this was about as good a look as he’d get.

He opened the door to find the two big cats staring up at him, and not too kindly, he thought. They stood their ground, and

Shanahan stepped over them, hoping they wouldn't crawl up his inseam.

"I think I saw your wife get on a plane for Detroit this morning," Shanahan said. "You have relatives there?"

Marty's face went red immediately. "Get the fuck outta here."

Shanahan was sure that if he was doing nothing else, he was stirring things up, perhaps wrecking a marriage. Perhaps Helen was having a little affair in the Motor City. The phone book in the Nora Library, not too far from Marty's place, yielded a Howard Cross Private Investigating Service downtown on Pennsylvania Street.

Shanahan had never heard of it. The company had a small ad that, aside from the name, address, and phone number, said "Honest, discreet, effective, and inexpensive."

The building was across from the World War Memorial, a massive edifice dedicated to the war dead, something that the conservative midwestern city did better than any other city except perhaps Washington, D.C. The building he went into was built sometime in the thirties, Shanahan guessed, and had its lobby redone twenty years ago.

He looked at the directory. There it was under H for Howard, just above "Indiana Civil Liberties Union."

Shanahan went to the sixth floor, passed by the ICLU's modest digs and down a long, narrow hall. The only thing they had done to this floor since they built it was paint the wood trim white, put in cheap carpet, and install ugly light fixtures that cast an unfortunately bright and ugly fluorescent green everywhere.

The office was just that. An office. A room with a desk in it. And behind the desk was the man Shanahan presumed to be Howard Cross.

"Howie," the guy said after Shanahan inquired. He stood up behind his cheap desk, offered his hand. "It was a cute name in high school," he said apologetically. "Of course, I was a cute guy." He had put a paperback down as he stood. *The Restaurant at the End of the Universe.*

Howie was maybe thirty-five, if you looked carefully beyond the cultured tan. He had blond, curly hair and looked to be in shape—maybe a lifeguard in a former incarnation.

"A modern day Sam Spade," Shanahan said. He'd never read it, but he saw the movie three times. Not because it was a detective movie—he didn't like detective movies—but because he liked Bogart. He never liked pretty heroes.

"I got the transom," Howie said, looking up at the door behind Shanahan, "but you're not exactly what's supposed to come through the door."

"But an attractive blonde did, didn't she, a day or so ago?"

"What can I do for you?" Howie said, dodging the question.

"Information," Shanahan said.

"About what?"

"Who."

"Who then?" Howie said, staying patient, but looking carefully at Shanahan.

"A blond woman named Helen. A blue Miata convertible. A house in Meridian Hills. A husband named Marty who owns a strip joint."

"Sounds like you got a lot of information already. If you told me your name, I forgot it already."

"I want to know why she hired you." Shanahan sat down in the guest chair, an orange plastic shell on aluminum legs, something that looked like it belonged in the company cafeteria.

"I don't talk about clients. Who are you anyway?"

"I'd like to know why she hopped a plane for Detroit this morning and didn't bother to take along any luggage."

"You're not Marty Ray. You her dad or something?"

"Something."

Instead of getting angry, Howie Cross smiled, got real calm, relaxed. He sat on the edge of the desk.

"I'm not a hardass. Most people think I'm an okay guy. I don't mind trading information. But I like to know who I'm dealing with and why that person wants it. So we don't even begin to talk until I get the basics. And right after you tell me your name, you tell me how you know I'm working for Helen Ray."

Shanahan never read the newspapers. He distrusted them. When he had read them years ago as a form of defense against his wife—who somehow had the mistaken notion that reading the daily paper was a sacred time in a man's life—he realized that reporters and editors were just like other humans. More often than not they were lazy, bureaucrats no more interested in their work than order takers at second-rate hamburger chains or underpaid clerks at the local discount mart.

In newspapers, it's not always what's printed, it's what isn't. Truth is buried somewhere in the shadows of those grainy photos, hints at real life, clues to what happened, but never clear, rarely telling the whole story and often misleading.

He understood the media's complicity in the shaping of public views. Clearly he understood that in a city with a substantial black population, you could only expect to see blacks, males for the most part, represented in the newspapers as successes in sports and show business and failures in crime.

He clearly understood that the media, and particularly the newspapers in this city, could not only shape but nearly control the public perception of any issue. For that and countless other reasons, Shanahan didn't read the daily papers, foregoing even the coverage he'd get of the Cubs.

But he read them now, trying to keep track of the view the people of the city had of his two young clients. And there they were, mug shots of Leo and Billy, looking all the world in the flat light and the dismal reproduction like terrorists or rapists or mass murderers.

Below that was a picture of Lisa Dennison, a photo taken by the high school photographer, a photograph softly lit, delicate lace at her neck, the suggestion of a shy smile on her lips. Though the caption writer used the word "alleged" in the description, the girl was to any reader obviously still another victim of these brutal teenagers.

Below that was a photograph of Robert Silvers, the young, fiery, prematurely silver-haired prosecutor, a few stripes of the American flag in the background, saying that these weren't juveniles who committed these acts of violence and that they would be tried as adults. He was seeking the death penalty. He owed it to the people of the city, he said in the article, he owed it to the police department.

The story subtly alluded to his controversial personality and to what everyone knew: He was running for mayor.

The newspaper also had two other stories on Silvers. One was that he was asked to be the keynote speaker in Boston at some national gathering of city prosecutors. The other was a three-column story announcing a crackdown on gang-related activity focusing on the Arlington High School area and near Tech High School, John Marshall High School, and Woodruff Place.

Silvers had the keen sense to capitalize on media interest. He knew that it was in his best interest, publicitywise, to go after gangs when the news latched on to Billy and Leo. The newspapers and TV stations would have to bite and bite big on a related story.

Shanahan's reading was interrupted by a knock at the door. He slipped his glasses into a drawer in the desk and went to answer it.

"Swann."

The sound was muffled and Shanahan wasn't sure whether he heard the guy or read his lips but already knew it was the lieutenant. He'd seen his flat-topped head through the little window in the door.

After he let him in, Shanahan looked back out the door. No sign of other police, so he probably wasn't here to arrest him.

"A couple of pieces of news," Swann said, standing just inside the door.

"Sit down," Shanahan said, realizing it

sounded a little too much like an order and less like a proper host.

"No. It won't take long. The fire in the house where the kid burned was set by the owner. Poor guy, when he saw the police at his door, he couldn't talk. When he did start talking, he couldn't stop. Didn't know anybody was inside until we told him. Then he really fell apart."

"Insurance."

"Couldn't sell it. Couldn't afford to fix it up."

"That's not what the newspaper said this morning."

"We just found out."

Shanahan was sure the revised story, which would explain that charges for Lisa's murder would be dropped, would be placed in a few short paragraphs by the obituaries. The public would never know. The jury might not even be informed, and even if they were, it would hardly have the impact of those grisly photos of the kids, the innocent-looking victim, and the prosecutor who loved to use the phrase "family values."

"You said a 'couple' of things."

"Marty and Helen Ray have filed a complaint against you. Says you're harassing them? The next step is a restraining order. The step after that is an arrest. Why would you do something like that to those people?"

Swann's words came as they had before, a monotone. No inflection.

"Are you being cute, Swann, or are you dumb?"

Shanahan detected something that resembled a smile appear briefly on Swann's thin lips.

"I'm a homicide detective . . ."

"Is that supposed to clue me in? Dumb, then?"

Maureen entered the room, stopped on seeing Swann.

". . . and as a homicide detective, all I have are a bunch of facts. So far, the facts—the type of bomb, plastics, a sophisticated timer and an uncommon detonator—tell me that the explosion that killed Mrs. Ray's sister and her husband was a professional job. So far, the facts—a bayonet through the heart causing the heart to explode and splatter the walls and ceiling with blood—tell me that this wasn't a professional job."

"Would you like some coffee, Lieutenant Swann?" Maureen asked, suddenly acting like a housewife. "Shanahan made it."

"Sure," he said, and moved to the small upholstered chair Shanahan's wife used to sit in. No one else ever had. It looked small, delicate, and uncomfortable. Swann, a small and tidy man, seemed to fit the chair better than he fit his profession. Shanahan thought he looked like a funeral director, talked like a funeral director, precise and in calming tones.

Einstein hopped up on the policeman's lap suddenly. Swann didn't seem surprised or disturbed. He patted the cat's head, and Einstein curled up in his lap.

"Fact, Lieutenant Swann. Puckett was working on a drug deal that involved Sweethearts. Marty Ray owns Sweethearts. Puckett was having an affair with a supposedly rich woman, which was somehow connected to his work—work being the Sweetheart connection. Marty's wife, Helen, an attractive and by many standards a rich woman, left earlier today for a little day trip to Detroit."

Swann continued to pet Einstein as Shanahan talked. "A man is cheating on his wife," he said. "He gets run over by a car. Did God do it?"

"You lost me."

"Not everything is retribution. Not everything connects. Don't dismiss coincidence. Puckett was involved in dangerous work, true. For the purposes of his investigation he was living in a high crime area, not unknown for breaking and entering. Surprised burglars act irrationally sometimes. Marty Ray and his brother-in-law were allegedly dealing in cocaine. Also dangerous work."

Maureen handed him the coffee.

"Thanks," Swann said. "The two are connected only in the sense that some of the same players were involved in both."

"The same way you thought the little girl's death was at the hands of Billy and Leo?" Maureen asked.

"Yes," he said, not showing any signs that he'd been caught, then added, "Exactly."

"Do burglars carry around a bayonet when they break into houses?" Maureen asked.

"Not normally. But you'd be surprised what we find. Steel pipe, stun guns, butcher knives. Even found a slingshot once."

Einstein curled into a little circle. He was in Swann's lap for the long haul.

"And an experienced cop would let two kids stab him in the heart?" Maureen said. "He'd have to have seen it coming."

"Perplexing. But that particular bit of logic would also apply to anyone."

"Don't you think it even wise to find out who Puckett was sleeping with?" Maureen continued her line of questioning as if it were her case.

"Why?" Swann asked calmly.

"Woman scorned."

"There's already an arrest in that particular case. Circumstantial evidence, but enough of it for the prosecutor's office. I have to account for my time. The department isn't going to be too happy with me if I spend my time trying to undo a good bust."

Still he spoke without emphasis, as if there could be no question about it, serenely confident he was acting in accordance with the rules and that those rules were just and appropriate. But he looked away when he spoke about the department not being happy with him spending his time undoing the arrest. Then he turned back to Shanahan, his gaze meeting Shanahan's.

"If I were you, I wouldn't been seen in the vicinity of the Rays."

He put his coffee on the floor and gently picked up Einstein, putting him on the floor beside it. He got up. "Sorry, guy."

He turned to Maureen. "You think you'd be strong enough to plunge a blade three inches into a man's heart?"

"No sweat," Maureen said.

"Thanks," he said to Shanahan. "You make a good cup of coffee."

EIGHTEEN

Shanahan had been prepared to dismiss Jennifer Bailey as a suspect, primarily because the girl had been murdered. He could imagine her angry enough to kill Puckett; but not some little girl. And the last thing he imagined was Jennifer Bailey traipsing around an abandoned house with five gallon cans of gasoline.

Now she was back on the list. So was Helen Ray and/or perhaps Marty Ray. Though Puckett was obviously a bright cop, he would have considered Helen Ray to be a wealthy woman, as Shanahan did. She lived in the right neighborhood, had a trendy car, and may not have been too stingy with the money.

She may have found Puckett, a young, handsome guy, a pleasant diversion from

Marty Ray. Of course, it could be Marty Ray who discovered who was making his wife happy. Shit, it could have been the brother-in-law doing the business for Marty because Puckett was screwing the wife or because of the coke deals. If that were the case, Shanahan thought, it would be hell finding out, because the brother-in-law was dead. And nobody'd buy the story that the dead man did it, not with two live suspects who played so well in the newspapers at campaign time.

It was also logical to Shanahan that if Helen were, with or without her husband's knowledge, the coke pipe to Detroit, Puckett may very well have been on her tail in more ways than one. She discovered that before Puckett knew she discovered it, and killed him.

But there was still one more connection, one that he couldn't quite make. That was Connell. Why had he made such a big deal about getting the story on Billy and Leo, and why did he want to make the story a force in their conviction?

Too loose, he thought. He shook his head. "It's way out there," he said out loud.

"What's way out there?"

Shanahan laughed. "When you get old, you talk to yourself."

"Age has nothing to do with it," Maureen said. "I talk to myself all the time. Why, just a few minutes ago I said, 'Maureen, isn't it Shanahan's turn to cook?' And I said, 'It certainly is, Maureen, what do you suppose he's fixing?' "

Shanahan wondered if she would have even considered getting involved with him if he hadn't fixed dinner on their first date. She was a sensual being.

The phone rang and Maureen answered it. "Just a minute," she said. "It's somebody who wants to talk to my 'old man.' "

Shanahan wondered if it was Leo again. But it was Billy's calmer voice.

"Saw all these guys standin' in line to make a phone call, so I got in line and you was the only one I knew to call."

"How're things going?" There was quiet for a moment. "Billy?"

"Yeah. Pretty neat you sending me the comics. The guys here think I'm pretty weird."

"I didn't mean to get you in trouble."

"Just the opposite. Helps make me kinda untouchable, you know? Like at first I chewed on some soap and let it bubble outta my mouth. The guys don't know it's soap. They think I'm rabid or something, you know, a real freak, and they leave me alone."

"You see Leo?"

"No, they got us in different cell blocks now, like if we was together we'd break out. Just saw him today with the I lawyer. He didn't talk none, but his knuckles is all scabbed over."

"Did he look all right?"

"Looked like Leo."

"What'd the lawyer say?"

"Said we ought to be thinkin' about pleadin' guilty to keep our butts outta the chair. She didn't say it like that."

"What do you think about that?" Another long silence. Shanahan wasn't sure if he heard a sigh or not. "Billy?"

"Don't know what to think. Wasn't going nowhere in particular anyways. I mean maybe we should get some time for rippin' off the guy and some other shit we done. But I don't like people thinkin' we shivved this cop. I ain't that fucked up."

"I'm still working on it, Billy."

"Who's payin' you?"

"Nobody now. But that's not a problem."

"Why you doing it?"

"I know you didn't do it."

"That the reason?"

"Yeah."

"You're as weird as I am," Billy said. "I gotta go 'cause some dude with tattoos, no teeth, and bad breath is blowin' in my ear.

"One more thing, Billy. You and Leo told me that you watched Puckett's place and that he left at a certain time every day to go get some Mexican food."

"Yeah, down to Taco Bell. He left that day too. It's like somethin' outta *Nightmare Theater* or something. Fuckin' head trip."

"You were sure it was him?"

"Well, I thought a lot about it. I mean he always wore that stocking cap and that kind of Navy jacket with the buttons."

"The person you saw was black, then?"

"He kept his hands in his pockets. We wasn't right on top of him. I mean if we saw the dude wasn't black, then we'd've fuckin' figured it out."

Maureen was in bed beside him, but Shanahan could tell by her breathing she wasn't asleep. He wished that they would make love or talk about Hawaii or that he could get his mind in some clear place, but the phone call from Billy was disturbing. Shanahan didn't like the direction his mind was turning. Didn't like it at all.

Something nagged at him, and he was surprised that it hadn't been nagging earlier, angry that it hadn't because now it was too difficult to interrogate the kids. This mysterious stranger who allegedly wore Puckett's clothes and walked down the street away from the scene of the crime.

It had been evening, late hours of daylight when colors tend to gray out, Shanahan thought. And do you look at details such as the color of the little bit of flesh if the face is amidst the familiar clothing? One fills in the rest. Shanahan tried to remember whether Puckett was a dark-skinned or light-skinned black man.

Even he, trained to remember detail—though trained so long ago and lazy in those matters since—could not remember. But then newspaper photos were unreliable anyway. What he did remember was the room, the incredible amount of blood. How could a human have so much?

He had asked Billy and Leo before if they couldn't recollect something that didn't fit with the person walking out of the house and the man they had watched for days. Shorter? Taller? Heavier?

They couldn't come up with anything, no feeling that something was wrong that could be traced to the posture of the person leaving or the pace of the walk. But they would be high on adrenaline if nothing else. Details would slip, this was the day they would break in and steal, an act that for many was as exciting in the doing as it was rewarding in the material sense.

They would be fooled because they wanted it so badly. But Billy was cool. Shanahan had seen it. Cool the way he held the revolver on Lieutenant Swann and his men, cool when he was caught. Cool enough to kill the policeman? Could Puckett's machismo have extended, as Harry suggested, so far that he thought he could bluff a couple of kids?

Could Leo have had such a blind machismo himself that he wouldn't back down on a dare? Yes. Like the comic book X-Men themselves, Shanahan thought, self-defined mutant kids dress up for the burglary, ninja style or fantasy style. The blood splatters their costumes, not their everyday clothes. The person they say was walking away was part of their, probably Billy's, creation. That's how Billy thought, quick and clever.

If there was such a person, then that person must have known Puckett's moves every bit as well as Billy and Leo did. He or she would have had to have chased his moves as well. Why wouldn't Billy and Leo have noticed someone else watching their own prey?

Shanahan shook his head. He didn't want this idea to make sense. He remembered the stories of young, very young, Viet Cong children with hand grenades. The prisons were full of teen murderers.

Maybe he'd been soft, Shanahan thought, a sort of creeping grandfatherism, soft-hearted, soft-headed sentimentality creeping in.

"Maybe they did do it," Shanahan said to Maureen as they lay in bed.

"The kids? No," she said.

"Why not? This shadow character who dresses up in Puckett's clothes has a touch of fantasy to it."

"Did they find the clothes?"

"No. But they could have been destroyed or hidden, or maybe they didn't exist in the first place."

"He was found naked, didn't you say?"

"No," Shanahan laughed. "He was wearing a suit, and as far as I know, his genitals were still intact."

"That was kind of her," Maureen said.

"That's what I mean. He was wearing a suit. He wasn't even in undercover garb. And what in the hell do you mean 'her'? You can't assume that yet."

Maureen turned on the light, sat up in bed. "It's an old game."

"What is?"

"What we're going to do. Just do as I say quickly. Look at your fingernails."

Shanahan made a fist, turned it over and looked at his nails.

"So?"

"Okay, now get out of bed. Go on, stand up."

"No. What are you doing? This is stupid."

"Do it," she said. "There's a reason."

"This is stupid," Shanahan said, getting out of bed, standing there naked while Maureen looked on. She gave a little look.

"How does it feel to be a sex object?"

Shanahan started back to bed. "That's it, Maureen."

"No, no, no, no. Now, c'mon. That's a little side point. You know, it's how you look at me sometimes. But wait." She was enjoying herself. "Pick a foot and look at the bottom of it, the sole."

"What?"

"You're being difficult. Just do it."

Shanahan lifted a foot, then reached down and grabbed his ankle, almost painfully twisting an ankle, and looked down. He nearly lost his balance.

"Where is all this going?"

"One more thing," Maureen said as she slid out of bed, Shanahan glancing at her bare ass as she escaped through the door. When she came back, she handed him a book of matches.

"Strike a match. This is the last one, I promise."

Shanahan pulled a match from the book, struck it, held it up with a mawkish grin for her to see, then flicked his wrist to put it out.

"Okay, now you can get in bed."

"Thank you," he said, climbing in. "Thank you very much."

She moved up close to him. "Now, when a woman looks at her nails she usually holds her hand straight out, palm down, like this. She doesn't usually make a fist. When a woman looks at the soles of her feet, she lifts the leg up behind her and looks over her shoulder. When a woman strikes a match she does it the way she's supposed to, striking the match away from herself not toward herself the way you did, and when she extinguishes the flame, she usually blows it out and doesn't show off the way you did."

Shanahan was quiet. Maureen waited.

"All right," he finally said, "assuming you are right, what does that have to do with anything?"

"I read the coroner's report," she said.

"Okay," he said, nodding, suggesting she might want to complete her thought because it still made no sense to him.

"The angle of the knife . . ."

"Oh shit," Shanahan said. "It came down into his heart."

"Yep," she said. "Down. Sounds like a very mad female, Detective Shanahan."

"It's pretty flimsy."

"It seems like all the guys in the movies who stab other guys stab the victim in the stomach. They hold the knives low and if anything they stab up, not down." Her voice trailed off a bit, as if some thought suddenly disturbed her confidence.

"That's street fighting. Gangs."

"Yeeeeeyeah, I know. Wouldn't that be the way Billy and Leo would do it? Like street gangs or guys in the movies? It seems like the only time a guy comes down with the blade is when it's in the back."

"This is the movies, you're talking about."

"Yeah, I know," she said.

"It sounds pretty sexist."

"That too." She smiled.

"I'm not sure I'm comfortable with the scientific method you're using here."

"But Shanahan, you bought it at first. Your instincts were just the same as mine."

"Yeah," he said, suddenly tired. Was he trying to bail out on Billy and Leo right after he had told Billy he believed they didn't do it? He was disgusted with himself He was disgusted with Jennifer Bailey as well for not slowing down the trial. He almost hoped she was the one.

"I have other instincts right now. You want to mess around?"

"Maureen . . . uh . . ."

"It's all right."

"Where are you going now?" Shanahan asked Maureen, who was running out of the bedroom.

"Ice cream. Want something?"

He didn't hear her come back to bed.

NINETEEN

The next morning Shanahan got a call from Harry.

"Impossible," Harry said.

"What's impossible? The car?"

"This is the deal, Deets. You got to know the address, then you can find out who owns it. Don't work the other way around."

"No other way?" Shanahan wasn't surprised. He knew that was the way it was set up ten years ago when he was trying to find out what somebody owned. But he thought with computers they'd have things cross-referenced.

"That's the way the government bureaucrats set up their records. Look, I went to some of the garages yesterday, you know, just drove around. Nothin'. Hell, the police probably got the word out, and with all the cops drivin' around spottin' nothin', then I figure it's been repainted, driven out of town or driven in a river somewhere."

"Thanks, Harry. You own the bar yet?"

"Paperwork, Deets. You was right about

having to prove I'm no kinda crook or somethin'. Can I ask you somethin'?"

"Sure."

"Why am I lookin' at Connell's property?"

"I'm not sure. It's a real loose connection, but one I have to checkout."

"You talk to the guy?" Harry asked.

"Not yet, but I plan on it."

"Him? Himself? You gonna actually talk with the man one on one?"

There was no doubt that after forty-some-odd years of friendship there were things about Harry that Shanahan didn't care for. One of them was this general acquiescence to class. Harry was that way in the Army, the higher the rank, the more in awe Harry was.

It was Harry's unspoken contention that there are two classes of people. One of them was where most everybody was, and that class included everyday Joes—from suburban housewives to factory workers to the homeless and the nickel-and-dime criminals. The other class was inhabited by people other people talked about or saw in the news.

And while Jim Connell was no Donald Trump, not even as high in that category as you could go in Indianapolis—there were others, bankers, real estate developers, certainly the multimillionaire monopoly owners of the two daily papers who not only had money, but real clout—Connell was talked about. Popping up on the newscasts, in the papers, and quite often in the local business newspaper, a weekly noted for either sensationalizing the trivial or trivializing the sensational.

"Yes, I am going to meet the great one, Harry, right after I interview Queen Elizabeth, the Prince of Monaco, and some guy named Christ, first initial, J."

"Yeah, yeah, I know. He puts his pants on the same way I do. But he puts on a better pair of pants, Deets. And he wears them to—"

Shanahan didn't want to get into that argument again. "Okay, and we both know he gets a pricier coffin when he buys it. Right?"

"Right," Harry said. "He do it?"

"I don't think so. Maureen has me convinced it's a woman."

"Look, you know something, don't you? Your kids don't have a chance. I been following it in the papers and on TV and talking around, you know."

One thing about Harry's class system: It's shared by more people than not, and Shanahan had never doubted Harry's barometric ability, his canny talent to reflect the attitudes of the public at large. He'd never lost a bet on a presidential election, including Harry Truman's victory over Thomas Dewey.

"That doesn't make it right," Shanahan said with an anger that surprised even him.

"Deets?"

"What?"

"I'm being followed," Harry said.

Shanahan fed the animals, watched Maureen drive off to the bookstore to pick up a real estate book that was recommended by another real estate book she'd just finished reading. When English called, Shanahan stopped pacing and settled in behind his desk.

"Nobody knows," English said. "The art director says that Sarah must have something on him. Otherwise he can't imagine how she got the money to buy him out, and besides, Connell wasn't too happy about selling."

Shanahan was never keen about speculation, especially from employees about their employers. But it made some sense. He asked English if he had noticed anyone following him.

"You're kidding."

"Probably, but check it out anyway." He filled the young reporter in on what he'd discovered and, more aptly, what he hadn't.

The next phone call came from Howie Cross. It was unexpected. When Howie agreed to exchange information rather than give it, Shanahan finally told him who he was and what he wanted to know, including Helen's and perhaps Marty's possible mob connections. And Howie explained that he was on the case to discover who blew up her sister and that his employment lasted for about an hour and a half. She hired him, drove home, called him back and took him off the case.

This conversation with Howie was unexpected and brief.

"I'm being followed. Two dudes in a blue Buick. Could be the cops, could be another detective agency, could be the mob. How's that for fun? All starting after your visit."

"Maybe it's one of your other clients," Shanahan suggested.

"I don't have any other clients."

It was a similar but not exact duplicate

of Harry's description. A plain sedan. Harry's was green, however. Speculation was added to speculation. Whoever it was had enough manpower to tail two people at the same time. At least.

When Shanahan hung up, he merely sat at his little desk in the living room, looking out of the screen door leading to the backyard. Casey was stretched out under the desk and Einstein had now picked that little chair of his wife's which Swann had sat in, as his favorite chair. He was curled and asleep, his ear twitching every sixty seconds or so.

What do they dream? Do they dream of chasing mice? Maybe of being chased by dogs? Sex? Shanahan wondered, but only for a moment. Einstein's dreams probably took place in the kitchen and had something to do with the sound of a can opener.

It was one of those days that moved quickly from gray to sunny and back to gray again.

"Why them and not me?" Shanahan asked himself about the guys following his cohorts. Then it occurred to him that both his friend Harry and his fellow P.I., Howie, had simply been more alert. He had simply not thought about being followed and had obviously not been looking in his rearview mirror.

"I'm getting sloppy, Casey." He wondered if that's how it was, getting older. These kind of things, things he had been so good at simply slip away, mostly unnoticed. Funny you don't think of yourself getting older, he thought.

He figured who he was now was pretty much the same Shanahan as he was when he was twenty. No, more than that, he laughed, the same person he was in the third grade. People don't change, not the basics. If anything, you just get more pronounced and learn to hide the things you need to hide to get along. But nothing changes.

He tried picturing Maureen in the third grade. It wasn't difficult. She'd no doubt have an ice cream cone and flirt with the kids in the seventh grade. She did like older men.

Shanahan picked up the phone and called English to set up a time with Connell.

English was out. So, apparently, was Connell, but he got the number of Connell's office and dialed.

"You've reached the offices of Connell,

Baines and Hollyfield. If you know the extension, you may enter the number at any time during this message. If you do not know the extension, please push the pound sign for the company directory."

"I don't have a pound sign!" Shanahan exclaimed, realizing he still had not changed from a rotary dial despite a dozen letters from the telephone company, some offering to switch him for free.

The voice sounded like the voice at the United Airlines terminal at O'Hare. Was the person real?

"If you wish to speak to the operator instead, please push zero. You may do so now."

He dialed zero, though he was pretty sure it wouldn't work. It didn't.

He took a shower, put on his one suit, black and stodgy. The white shirt was starched and uncomfortable, and his tie was either too wide or too thin, he wasn't sure which, but knew he hadn't had the right tie width in twenty years. He took his suit off in disgust, then put it back on again. It was important to get past the receptionist.

Maureen was coming in as he was going out.

She was shocked. "You look like you're ready for your . . . going to a funeral."

Shanahan knew what she had started to say. Death was on her mind.

"It's okay," she said. Then changing the subject, "I stopped by O'Malia's and got some ice cream, and they had these melons I never heard of and then a bunch of other stuff. I got carried away."

Shanahan checked the street, but saw no car that was suspect. By the time he got on Washington Street heading west toward downtown, he saw a number of plain cars that would fit with Howie's and Harry's observations. But only one of them had two guys dressed in suits. Shanahan guessed it was the big Ford, though he had long lost track of the new car models. It was black.

He would like to have gotten behind them, check out the plate. He slowed and pulled into a car parts store, hesitated by the side of his car to see if they'd pass, but they turned the street before and he couldn't see that far.

The last thing he wanted to do was let them know he knew they were there. If he was sure they were police, he'd go up to them. If they were representing somebody else, he didn't want the confrontation.

He went inside and asked the guy behind the counter if he had a fan belt for a '72 Chevy Malibu.

"You kiddin'? A 'seventy-two? Put it on order, fifteen days," the guy said.

The offices of Connell, Baines and Holyfield were on the fortieth floor of a building shaped like a box of Nabisco Saltines set on end. It was chrome and glass and looked no better to Shanahan now than it did when it was built.

It was ostensibly headquarters for a major bank, but they had subleased many of its floors. The businesses, as he examined the directory, all had combination names, names that might have meant something if he had cared to keep track of rising and falling local celebrities the way Harry did.

The fortieth floor belonged to Connell and to the two who had second and third billing. The lobby was paneled in a deep reddish wood. Chairs, high backs with wings, stood beside a fireplace, a real one, it seemed to Shanahan. A fireplace in a high rise? A pretty expensive piece of engineering, considering there were a few more floors above this one. Over the fireplace was a traditional landscape painting of a creek, a high cliff, and trees. Ten feet from the chairs was an ample sofa, which was where Shanahan waited after checking in with the receptionist, who sat behind a paneled half wall, very much like a judge's bench, only shorter.

Shanahan had been surprised that Connell had agreed to meet with him without an appointment. So was the receptionist, it seemed.

"I'm sorry to keep you waiting," the man said. He was smallish, trim. The face seemed older than his hair. There was no smile, but no evidence of impatience, no indication that Shanahan was a bother. They shook hands and Connell suggested they talk in his office, which as it turned out was larger than Shanahan's house.

Essentially it was three rooms open to one another at the corner of the fortieth floor. Two of them had views, one of other tall buildings, the other noting the flatness of the city by looking north. Entire neighborhoods were visible in geometric patches of the city. Shanahan followed Connell across either a Persian or oriental rug, past a large table with several chairs, to two chairs intimately close to one another.

Behind them was the desk, a massive chunk of intricately carved wood that seemed out of keeping with the rest of the furniture and was remarkably free of debris. Perhaps it had been his father's desk. Shanahan continued to look out the windows before sitting.

"I do the same thing," Connell said. "Every morning I marvel at what this city has become in the last twenty years or so. You're from here, aren't you, Mr. Shanahan?"

"Yes. Last few decades."

"Then you'll remember what a deserted ugly place the downtown was in the sixties? Not that we don't have our problems still."

Connell sat, and Shanahan sat as well, uneasily.

"I'm surprised you allowed me to see you," Shanahan said.

"Oh? Why would you feel that way?"

Suddenly Shanahan felt very uncomfortable. Somehow, the element of surprise that would reveal something of the man had worked not against the man, who seemed altogether too comfortable, but against him.

"You're a busy man," Shanahan said, "and you don't know me."

"My wife said you stopped by, but she didn't say why. I believed that you must have something important to tell me, otherwise you would not have gone out of your way to have a word with me."

"Well, yes. Your wife was very kind. I'm a private detective, Mr. Connell."

"I see. I don't believe she told me that."

Shanahan detected a slight loss of composure pass over Connell's face. A break in the little mask of civility. Apparently Mrs. Connell wanted her husband to twist in the wind a bit. Shanahan thought that was a wise tactic. He remained quiet. If she hadn't told Connell who he was, it was also apparent she didn't mention anything about why he wanted to talk to her husband.

"Maybe I can save you some trouble here. Like many men, Mr. Shanahan, I've had my share of indiscretions, and because I have a remarkable wife, she has endured them, knowing full well that they would pass."

Connell raised his eyebrows as if he'd just completed his move in a chess match or served a little green ball over the net. Shanahan turned away from the expectant Connell and stared out the window.

"Loosely translated, Mr. Shanahan, that means she knows."

This time the words were tough, combative. Connell's eyes narrowed and looked into his.

Shanahan had been impressed. He had even thought that maybe Harry was right about the rich and powerful, had it not been for Connell's willingness to answer questions he hadn't been asked.

"I'm not here to blackmail you, Mr. Connell."

"What am I to suppose?" Connell had trouble with his earlier tone of gentle giant. "You stop in, visit my wife at our home. Unannounced. Then you just drop by my office."

"She didn't tell you, then?" Shanahan said, knowing full well she hadn't.

"What?"

"I'm investigating the murder of the undercover policeman, Samuel Puckett."

Connell's eyes opened wide. "What in God's name do you think I know about this?"

Shanahan knew that question would be asked. And he didn't have an answer. "I don't want to disclose that right now," he said. He certainly didn't want to talk about the magazine now. There was no reason to compromise English, for two reasons. One, he didn't want to risk the boy's job, and two, he might continue to need English as a source.

Connell stared.

"Perhaps I'll be able to talk about how I came to know your involvement," Shanahan continued trying to bluff, "at some later meeting." He wasn't particularly good at telling lies, and wondered if Connell was good at picking them out. Probably not; he believed that Connell was too angry to be observant.

Connell stood. "This is absurd. This is a police case. They've made an arrest."

Shanahan stood, knowing his interview had come to an end—and that was fine. All he expected was to take the measure of the man and let him know there just might be some loose ends. "They've arrested two kids whom I represent," he said, wondering where he picked up the "whom"—sometimes his words surprised him. "They didn't do it. And I can prove it."

"Is that some sort of threat?"

"Go figure," Shanahan said. "I can find my way out." He glanced out the window as he headed for the door. The words "lord of all he surveys" came to mind. Perhaps James Connell was the dim bulb that his wife and employees thought he was. Harry wouldn't like that.

TWENTY

The black sedan picked up Shanahan shortly after the green Malibu exited the garage on Ohio Street. They knew what they were doing, following discreetly a couple of cars behind.

Shanahan ignored them. After the smugness wore off regarding his conversation with Connell, putting the scare of Jesus into the chief executive, Shanahan realized he'd really gotten no new information. There was nothing to link Connell with the murder, besides his own gut feeling.

What he'd like to do is find out who Connell was playing house with, see if that led anywhere. But he'd like to get rid of his new friends first.

When he got back to the house, he put in a call to Lieutenant Swann. Swann was out, but Shanahan left word for him to return the call. He thought about calling Rafferty, but Rafferty would be irritated and probably wouldn't know anyway.

Surprisingly, the return call came within ten minutes.

The voice on the other end said, "This is Swann. What's up?"

"You having me and a couple of felons I associate with followed?"

"Nope. You're at home, I take it?"

"Yeah."

"Are they outside? Can you see them?"

Shanahan had already checked. "They're too good for that."

"It's probably not us, then. You get the plate?"

"Couldn't," Shanahan said, "without making it obvious. It's a black car. Ford, I think."

"Hmmm. Who else are they following?"

"A friend of mine, Harry Stobart, and a P.I. named Howie Cross."

"You pals with Howie?" Swann asked. As always with Swann, there wasn't a hint of surprise, disapproval or approval.

"You know him?" Shanahan asked. Two could play that game.

"Stick around," Swann said. "It may take a while, but I'll call you back."

Shanahan played his answering machine.

The first message was from Maureen. She had decided to go to her father's funeral. She'd be back tomorrow night. The second message was from Mrs. Dunfy, who was suing her husband for divorce and would have to rely on Shanahan's testimony. The third message was from Mr. Dunfy, who said he was going to sue Shanahan for character assassination, fraud, and breaking up his marriage.

The fourth call was from Howie Cross.

"What I did was"—it was Howie's recorded voice—"buy this 'seventy-eight Olds from my brother for fifty bucks, let these nerds follow me around, get 'em just where I want 'em, then swerve in front of 'em and step on the brakes."

Howie Cross was laughing.

"After calling me more names than I ever heard strung together, they vanished. The car's a rental. I'll track it down, but Shanahan, they ain't cops of any kind, not state, fed or city. Expensive suits that look cheap, Detroit accent, unless I miss my guess, and real pissed. One guy had blood coming out of his nose, the other guy messed up his hand or something. By the way, you don't owe me a fifty or nothing. My pleasure. I'll get back with you."

Shanahan called Swann. He didn't tell him how Howie Cross came to the conclusion, but told him that Cross was pretty sure they weren't cops and that they looked mob to him.

"Howie ought to know," Swann said.

"So you know Cross?"

"You could say that," Swann said.

"What else could I say?"

"He's your kind of P.I., Mr. Shanahan."

"What's that supposed to mean?"

"Well, he was on the police force for a while, vice, was asked to leave because he didn't want to arrest anybody. Then he went to work for a big security firm and he didn't like how they did business and told them that and they waved bye-bye. If you have to do things your way, you usually have to do them by yourself."

As always, there was no accusation in Swann's observations.

"He's a good man," Swann said.

"From your earlier conversation, I gather I'm on my own with these guys."

"No," Swann said quickly and firmly.

Shanahan was glad Maureen decided to go to the funeral. Not being there might be a source of later regret for her. For Shanahan, it got her out of the way in the event things got nasty.

Swann's plan was simple. Both Shanahan and Harry would travel separate prescribed routes at prescribed times. When the police, in unmarked cars, picked up the tail, they would simply pull them over.

It was doubtful, Swann had said, they could hold them, but they could run a check on their ID's, and if they were lucky would find them armed, and bring charges if they did not have permits to carry.

Shanahan did as he was instructed, watching in his rearview mirror as the flashing lights temporarily affixed to the top of three plain sedans pulled over the fourth sedan. He resisted the urge to turn around and help conduct the interrogation. Swann had been clear on that matter.

Things were going better until he got home, waited two hours, and called Swann. Swann thanked Shanahan for his help but was evasive about what he'd learned, and Shanahan got his second cautionary lecture about how the two cases—the bombing of Dierdorf's Lincoln and the death of Puckett—were separate and would be treated as such by the police department.

Again, he felt that Billy and Leo's case was at a standstill. There was nothing, just a nagging notion that James A. Connell was somehow involved.

Shanahan fed the animals and decided to take his troubles to Delaney's, where he witnessed two disturbing scenes—one was owner-to-be Harry trying to learn how to make a frozen daiquiri, and the other was the appearance of Jennifer Bailey's face on the big-screen TV saying she was prepared for the trial which would begin Monday. Not only that, but Robert Silvers was going to prosecute—personally.

"The only reason I'm pleading not guilty, Mr. Shanahan, is because Silvers refuses to plea-bargain," Jennifer Bailey said in her office when Shanahan arrived and barged into a conference she was having with two young men in gray suits.

"Then we have something to thank the prosecutor for," Shanahan said.

"Look, I'm in the middle of a meeting," she said, nodding to the two young gentlemen.

"Are they facing death by electrocution, Ms. Bailey?"

"Mr. Shanahan . . ."

"If they're not, then ask them to get out."

"Listen, Mister, uh . . ." the thin, balding one said.

"I said get out," Shanahan said to him, then fixed his stare on the other.

"Perhaps we could finish this at another time, Ms. Bailey," said the other, getting up slowly, making his little pile of papers neat and tucking them into an attaché case.

"I'm very sorry," Jennifer Bailey said, "this is just very unfortunate."

"I completely understand," said the man packing his case. "Henry," he turned to the blond, "this is something we can work up some preliminaries on and then get back with Ms. Bailey."

"You're a very rude man," Bailey said to Shanahan when the men had left.

"What in the hell are you going to defend them with? You've admitted as much by saying you were willing to plea-bargain to *what* offense? For what sentence? What in the hell could you be thinking?"

Jennifer Bailey sat down at the large, now empty conference table. Only a small stack of papers sat before her. She looked more tired and defeated than angry.

"If we wait, and I'm not sure we could if we wanted to, the story will only get worse. Worse for Billy and Leo, worse for any possible defense of them. The public is irate, but not as irate as they can get if Silvers is allowed to use this as campaign fodder over the next several weeks.

"Right now," she said slowly and calmly, as if trying to convince herself as much as Shanahan, "we can point up a number of things: One, as you explained, there was no evidence of blood on the defendant's clothing, no prints on the weapon, and the fact that an experienced police detective put up no apparent defense."

"You know better than I do," Shanahan said, also slowly and calmly, though unlike Bailey, he did so to keep from exploding in anger, "they have the money transaction, an eyewitness who puts them at the scene before, during, and after the crime, prints in the room, and you've already noted they're not exactly the Waltons. It looks to me like you're doing everything you can to help them get railroaded—right into the chair."

"What we can present is enough evidence that will cause the jury to have sufficient doubt . . ."

"Beyond a shadow of a doubt is what they say, isn't it?"

"That's not what I'm saying. The jury will convict them Mr. Shanahan. Of that I have little doubt."

Shanahan felt like he'd swallowed his stomach. "That's one helluva defense!"

"What I'm trying to explain is that a jury will be hard-pressed to put two kids to death."

"You're going to trial and that's all you have? That's all you hope for?"

"Yes, Mr. Shanahan, unless your heroic and brilliant efforts in uncovering the real murderer have met with success?"

Again she had turned it around.

"And I don't see any sign that your expensive and reputable, didn't you say, private investigation firm came up with anything," he said angrily. "Or are you holding out their spectacular findings?"

"No. They found nothing we can use. I'm sorry I belittled you earlier . . . I mean about being professional."

"It didn't hurt for long," Shanahan said dryly, "but I am convinced, Ms. Bailey, that it was a woman who killed Samuel Puckett, and I'm further convinced that it was a woman of color." He reached in his coat pocket for the ripped photo he had taken from Puckett's apartment, but decided not to show it to her now. "And I don't intend to see them juiced."

He studied her for a reaction, but there was only a blank stare.

"I asked you, do you understand me?"

"You still don't believe me, do you? I didn't kill Samuel Puckett." She said this flatly, no anger, no plea, nothing contrived to convince him in her tone. "And if you have me disqualified, Mr. Shanahan, and I'm replaced by a public defender, you will have sent those boys to their deaths. So, unless you can be absolutely sure you can find out who did it in whatever time you get by the disqualification delay, I'd be very careful about what you do with me for their sakes."

"I'll think about it," he said. "How much time do I have?"

"It will all happen quickly. There's not a lot to present."

"I already figured that out, Ms. Bailey." Nothing she said was going to be encouraging, and Shanahan tried to quell his anger. "Can you give me an estimate? In days? In hours?" he added sarcastically.

"A day for jury selection. Silvers will grandstand a bit with an opening statement and follow it with experts, coroner, fingerprinting and so on." She closed her eyes, seemed to be counting. "Five, I think. There will be Price and one or two neighbors, the arresting police, the police involved in the drug and money scheme. Two days for the prosecution. That's three."

"And you. How long will you take?"

She bowed her head. "There are no witnesses for the defense."

"No experts who can say something about the height of the assailant? No one you can call on to testify about how the blood would have to have gotten all over the killer? Nothing? This is it?"

"Yes, there are some things I can do. But I'm afraid it isn't much and I don't know how long I can drag it out."

"What about Billy and Leo? Don't you think the jury could hear their story?"

"Put them on the stand and we'll lose any possibility the jurors will find them too young to bear the consequences of their actions."

"What consequences. Send them to Plainfield for burglary? They didn't kill anyone. You keep forgetting that."

"Dear God, Mr. Shanahan, don't you see it yet?" She seemed on the verge of tears. "It's done. Whether they did it or not doesn't make any difference. Not your car theory, not your blood-splattering theory, not your other woman theory. Nothing is more important now than keeping them alive. If my strategy is to prove their innocence, they'll die. My strategy has to be to keep them away from the death sentence, and I'm not even sure I can do that."

Shanahan broke the long sticks of vermicelli in half and tossed them in the pot of boiling water. This was his staple—pasta, butter and garlic—before Maureen entered his life. Funny how old habits reinstate themselves so quickly.

Einstein meandered about on the countertop, always interested when Shanahan was in the kitchen. Shanahan's thoughts moved from the case to Maureen and back to the case again. Three days to solve a crime that as yet had too many leads, leading in too many directions.

While waiting for the pasta, Shanahan went out back, brought in the pot containing the rhododendron, a plant Maureen had bought. It was going to get cool tonight, maybe a frost. He'd cautioned Maureen against buying a plant that required special care. This was really a plant for a mild climate, doing its best in the tropics, not a midwestern plant subject to the vagaries of midwestern weather.

Shanahan took his plate of food to his desk, used the remote to flick on the TV. He checked out the sports channel. Tennis. He looked at his watch. It was nearing six P.M. He'd check out the local news. Einstein hopped up onto the desk. Einstein's life revolved around food. If he wasn't eating or trying to convince Shanahan to feed him, he'd sit and watch Shanahan eating. He kept his distance, sniffing the air.

"So what do I do now?" Shanahan asked. "Do I go for the long shot on Connell, concentrate on a delay by spilling the beans on Jennifer Bailey, push Helen and Marty Ray and go up against organized crime?"

He looked down at the rhododendron. On one shiny green leaf was a spider. It looked like a tiny ripe strawberry, a rich red body with long, pitch-black legs. It was, in its way, beautiful, elegant in a way one normally does not consider spiders.

At once he thought of Jennifer Bailey, her elegant long legs walking down Washington Street, wearing a stocking cap, a pea coat, and jeans on her way to Taco Bell. Jennifer Bailey, passionate enough to kill and clever and cool enough to cover it up. Jennifer Bailey, the other half of a torn vacation photo leaving Puckett, some sand and some sailboats. Jennifer Bailey, who removed herself coldly from Samuel Puckett's personal history, and him from hers as well, presiding over the fate of two kids who would take the fall.

The spider disappeared under a leaf.

The news on Billy and Leo was essentially the same as he'd seen earlier. When Robert Silvers's handsome face filled the screen, Shanahan paused. Perhaps there was a new development. But it was Silvers saying there were new leads in the bombing deaths of Mr. and Mrs. Dierdorf leads that connected the explosion with out-of-state organized crime. When the anchorwoman began talking about the proposed Circle Centre Mall, Shanahan flicked off the TV.

There had, of course, been no mention of Billy and Leo's case in the Dierdorf affair, and Shanahan was convinced that Swann was right. The prosecutor's office did not believe there was any connection, or if they did, it didn't fit in with Silvers's career plans.

Time was in short supply, yet Shanahan,

with an evening ahead of him, could not think of how to use it. There was so much to do, it seemed futile to do any of it. He would need to watch Helen, follow Connell, maybe check out Jennifer Bailey's digs—she was the only one who fit all the requirements.

She was a woman, had motive, access. He could imagine her with a knife and Puckett standing there laughing, convinced she wouldn't use it. She was also tall, and more important, black, which would fit with Billy and Leo's testimony about someone leaving the house they thought was Samuel Puckett.

But not only was there not enough time, there was not enough Shanahan to cover all the bases.

TWENTY-ONE

It was late when Shanahan decided to hire Howie Cross. How he'd pay Howie was another question. Somehow he'd get the money out of Rafferty. He'd not only need Howie, he'd have to call in Harry. He knew where to find Harry, and a quick look in the white pages told him where to find Howie Cross at home.

Howie Cross lived in a strange little house in the Butler-Tarkington area. Unlike the other homes, mostly handsome, well-kept, middle-class homes with character and lots of trees, Howie's place was way back from the street, hidden by growth untouched by a horticulturist.

There was a break in the growth, half lit by the street lamp, which also illuminated a beat-up red VW convertible.

Shanahan made his way up irregular stone steps that climbed a six-foot hill and down a long path which, judging by the feel under his feet, had some crushed stone but was now mostly earth.

Past the gate, which hung by one set of hinges and thus at an angle, Shanahan continued up the path to the door. Behind it he could hear strong blasts of rock 'n' roll, and wondered if he was about to interrupt a romance in progress.

"Yeah?"

"This is Shanahan," he said talking through the door. "I think I want to hire you."

"Can't talk business now," Cross said. The door opened slightly, and Howie, looking more than a little rough, poked his head in the narrow gap. "I'm about five sheets to the wind, which is two more sheets than what most people are when they're drunk on their ass or asses. I think it's asses because of the agreement with 'they.' Whatever, it's Friday night."

"I'm offering you work."

"I'm absolutely irresponsible in this condition." Howie stepped aside, opened the door, and Shanahan entered to find albums, clothing, magazines and dirty dishes strewn about as if some domestic tide had brought them there, scattering them willy-nilly on Howie Cross's personal beach.

"You got a trust fund or something, Howie?"

"I have two months of unopened bills in my desk drawer."

"Then let's talk now. You might not have an office, house, or phone tomorrow."

"Oh, using logic already in the relationship, are we?"

"I need you."

"The words I've longed to hear all my life, and I hear them from you."

Howie Cross stumbled across the living room, letting himself fall on the sofa, on top of a couple of layers of haphazardly discarded clothing, an empty bag of Doritos, and a couple of back issues of *Ring* magazine. He started to lean back, then leaned forward suddenly, his head on his knees. He was quiet. Had he passed out?

"Howie?"

"This is my listening posture. I figured you were gonna talk first."

There was more than a little thickness of speech, and Shanahan wondered if this was going to work out.

"You know James A. Connell?"

Another silence.

"Howie?"

"I'm thinking."

"Your thinking posture is a lot like your listening posture."

"You noticed that?"

"He's with Connell, Baines and Hollyfield."

"Is he with them now?"

"That's the name of the firm. Brokers, financiers, that sort of crap. Big man in the city."

"Yep, yep, yep. Now I remember. The civic father gig. Just takes a minute to get my head into the right game. I'm more comfortable with hookers and gamblers. Those are my kind of people, Shanahan, people without advertising and P.R. agencies, who are up front about screwing you."

"He has somebody he likes to sleep with besides his wife, and I'd like to find out who that is."

"She supposed to be that good?" he said, looking up.

"Howie."

"I know. I know. Something connected with the kids, right?"

"Yeah."

"You know, you come in here on Friday night and find out that not only am I a bad housekeeper but that I'm blitzed as hell. It's embarrassing. There's something I want you to know. And I want you to believe me. I'm always like this. There, I feel better."

"I appreciate what you did for me today," Shanahan said. "By the way, Lieutenant Swann says you're okay."

"You know Swann? He said that? The man is a walking rule book. No, I take that back. He's got the soul of a computer."

"He likes you."

"That's scary. You expect me to be able to sleep tonight?"

"I doubt if you'll have any trouble."

"So what do you want me to do? You want something to drink?"

Though it wasn't likely Connell would have a date on the weekend, Shanahan split Howie Cross and Harry Stobart's time watching Connell at ten hours each, beginning the next morning, Saturday. If nothing happened over the weekend, Shanahan decided, he would get English to provide information on Connell's daily schedule as best he could.

Meanwhile, he would do his best to get inside Jennifer Bailey's house or apartment, whatever she had, and do the same with the home of Marty and Helen Ray.

One bit of insight Howie Cross provided Shanahan was hopeful: he could always use Jennifer Bailey's conflict of interest later as a basis for a new trial, an appeal, or if needed, a stay of execution—should the worst happen in court.

What Howie Cross told him about Silvers, drawn from his brief tenure with the police department, jibed with the feelings a lot of people had about the prosecutor. His career was devoted to statistics. The conviction percentage to him was like a win and loss statistic for pitchers. And he wasn't particularly concerned about how he got them.

That was the essential difference between

Cross and Swann, who went through the academy at the same time. Swann believed in the system. Howie Cross didn't. When it came to the system, Shanahan was pretty much in Cross's camp.

Billy and Leo were caught in the system, a web of circumstantial evidence politically beneficial for a prosecutor ready for dinner.

As Shanahan expected, Saturday and Sunday brought nothing. He was unable to get a clear shot into the dwellings of Helen and Marty Ray or Jennifer Bailey.

Helen remained at the house all day Saturday, including the evening, when Marty pulled out of his garage in his Mercedes, no doubt heading for Sweethearts. Sunday, she left for awhile in the afternoon and came back with shopping bags from the Fashion Mall.

And Jennifer, who lived in a fine old home on upper Washington Boulevard, ran errands on Saturday. Dry cleaning, grocery shopping, leaving a young man outside puttering around the lawn. On Sunday she stayed home. Shanahan hoped she was working on the defense.

Harry and Howie both failed to score as well. Harry, who took the daylight hours, had checked the Connell house for back entrances and, finding none, settled in down the road from the great gate. Visitors came on Sunday, family presumably, stayed the afternoon and left in the early evening. Howie's sting was even less worthwhile.

Howie told Shanahan he wasn't surprised. His six years on vice led him to believe that unfaithful spouses were rarely unfaithful on weekends. They were weekend husbands and wives, he said, and Wednesday swingers.

It was easier to make excuses during the week, either managing to squeeze a little squeeze, as he put it, during the workday or calling home and saying it was necessary to work late. Don't wait up, honey.

Maureen came back on Sunday night, tired but not as depressed as he imagined she'd be. She had a letter from her father, she said, that she would read sometime. To Shanahan the way she said "sometime" could be translated as "decades from now."

Monday started off busy. At seven-thirty in the morning he received a summons to appear in court the following day. At first he thought it was about the Dunfy matter, the other cheating husband case. But it wasn't. He was to testify in Leo and Billy's trial. He had to read it twice to make sure he'd gotten it the first time. He was a witness for the prosecution. Fifteen minutes later Maureen received her summons.

It was clear to Shanahan that he and Maureen would be called upon to explain the night police found Billy and Leo at their place and to describe for the jury how they had drawn a weapon upon Lieutenant Swann and his fellow cops.

Not only could Shanahan not help them get off, he was being forced to help put them in and get them juiced.

At eight-thirty he received a telephone call from Lieutenant Swann.

"Thought you might like to know," Swann said with as much feeling as the woman who tells you what time it is on the phone, "we found the car."

"Where?"

"Key West, Dumont Street."

"Are you bringing it up?"

"Eventually," Swann said. "I know the trial is tomorrow, I'm testifying. But before you throw a tantrum, we had the Florida State Police dust the car for prints and run a vacuum on the carpet and upholstery."

"Yeah?"

"Don't get your hopes up either. They

found a lot of hair. Different hair, Shanahan. They found Caucasian hair, blond; Caucasian hair, black; and two different brands of hair owned by blacks. What does that suggest to you?"

It was the Caucasian black hair that threw Shanahan. He was convinced the blond hair belonged to Helen, but the dark hair suggested more than one person and might—he held on to the "might"—imply that both Billy and Leo had taken the car at least for a joy ride, and either drove it to Key West or, more likely, left the car somewhere, keys inside, and it was stolen by somebody else.

"It suggests that it might have been driven by Helen Ray and subsequently driven by someone else who took the car to Florida."

"That's not what it suggests to me," Swann said. "But we'll know soon. The various strands of hair are in an envelope and on a plane coming this way, but we won't have conclusive results until tomorrow afternoon at the earliest."

"Have you notified Jennifer Bailey?" If nothing else, the other sample belonging to a black might well connect her to the case.

"That's the prosecutor's job," Swann

said, "but I thought you might want to do it yourself in the event they're a little slow or decide they don't want to present it."

Well, what do you know? Shanahan thought, but didn't say it. "I appreciate it, Lieutenant Swann."

"You better put a hold on your appreciation. Who knows what side this will come down on?"

Shanahan dialed Jennifer Bailey's home number. There was no answer. He dialed her office, and the male voice explained she had been there and left for court.

TWENTY-TWO

Shanahan borrowed Harry's van, a ladder, and some paint buckets, brushes, and rollers. He drove by Bailey's house twice before pulling into the drive.

Inside, Jennifer Bailey's house was pretty much as Shanahan had expected. Though he had no particular interest or knowledge in interior design, as his own place would attest, he was pretty sure this was done well.

It was at once immaculate, ordered, and

comfortable, with strong hints of Japanese—a screen here, a scroll there. Simplicity dominated.

Her house was full of books, some in built-in bookcases on both sides of the fireplace, some of them neatly and, to Shanahan's eye, artistically stacked on the shiny wooden floors.

She had a whole series of books by Alan Watts and others clearly having something to do with Zen. He presumed the law books would be in another room. A woman like her would have an office in her home as well.

On the brown baby-grand piano there was a professionally taken photograph Shanahan recognized as Puckett, which sat just in front of a large, intricately carved Buddha.

Her refrigerator yielded contents similar to Puckett's—Japanese beer, for one thing, perhaps for him. Shanahan could imagine her elegant, long fingers playing piano but not wrapped around a bottle of beer, imported or not.

Among the regular stuff, mustard, mayonnaise, oranges, were packages of tofu, sushi contained in plastic pressure-sealed envelopes, and fish.

Like Puckett's, neither of the two bathrooms revealed any clues to physical or mental illness.

There were four bedrooms upstairs, one obviously lived in. On the night stand was a book a third of the way finished, or at least that's where it was marked. The title was *Nine Headed Dragon River: Zen Journals 1969–1982,* by Peter Matthiessen.

There was a bathroom on the other side of a dressing room off the bedroom. The bathroom gave up nothing but a couple of strands of hair on the brush by the makeup table, which Shanahan pocketed. The closets showed a wealth of fall and winter clothes. The labels in the clothing even had some names of people he'd heard of and they weren't Sears and Penneys.

Though he was sure the successful attorney was too smart to leave any signs about, he checked the hamper and looked at the soles of at least twenty-five pairs of shoes.

He went through her bureaus in the bedroom and dressing room as carefully as he could. Two other bedrooms were untouched and unlived in. The fourth bedroom stored her summer clothing. What hung in the closet was for the most part sealed in dry cleaners plastic, and most of it dated within the last two weeks. He took note of the dry cleaners' name.

He went through the drawers, mostly light sweaters and blouses. He wasn't finding what he was looking for, and he investigated the entire house, from basement to attic, for a cedar closet or chest. He didn't find what he was looking for.

The last room was the library or her office. It was a little darker and slightly more masculine. He glanced through her personal checkbook, quickly looked through the bills and stationery. Nothing struck him as unusual.

In the file drawer of the desk was a metal box. He had no trouble opening it, and found a small packet of correspondence tied in a silver satin ribbon.

These were letters, for the most part, Shanahan determined, from her mother, written in erratic, almost childish script. With them was a hand-painted photograph of a young couple. Judging by the style of clothing, probably taken in the forties, it was more than likely her parents.

The very last thing was Jennifer Bailey's passport, issued in 1983 and expiring in 1993.

Jennifer Bailey had been to France, Spain, and Japan.

Something was missing here as well.

Later Monday afternoon and into the evening, Shanahan checked the Ray house. People tended to notice someone sitting in a car or a van in these kinds of neighborhoods, so he found a house for sale two houses over and across the street. Harry was always prepared, and Shanahan used an old folding chair, placing it at the rear of the van and looking out of the back window.

Marty Ray came home at three-thirty in the afternoon and left again at eight P.M. Helen was still there. He'd seen her drive her little blue Miata in the garage earlier. Shanahan prayed she wasn't settling in for a Home Box Office double feature. He had to get inside. Of course he would settle for some bloodstained clothing or bloodied shoes belonging to either Marty or Helen, though the latter was where Shanahan would put his money.

Shanahan would also settle for something that would link her to James Connell, a farfetched notion, but one he was thinking a lot about. Helen Ray was an unlikely love match for the likes of Connell, but stranger things happened all the time. No one in their right minds would have put him and Maureen together either.

By nightfall Shanahan was grouchy and hungry. The chair was uncomfortable. It was boring as hell, and he had forgotten lunch and had stubbornly and stupidly resisted Maureen's sensible suggestion he take some sandwiches with him. The thing was, he knew better. He'd camped out on streets looking for wayward husbands more times than he'd care to count.

The only thing he'd brought with him was a thermos, but he'd drained the last of his coffee two hours before. He searched the van and found Harry prepared here too—a bottle of Coke, a can of honey-roasted peanuts, a flashlight, and lo and behold, a pair of binoculars.

At roughly nine-thirty, his stomach satisfied with Coke and peanuts, Shanahan saw lights go on in the far room. He picked up the binoculars, focused them through the vertical shades, and saw Helen Ray, blond hair down, her beautiful naked body appearing and disappearing in a dance without music with a peach-colored towel.

He lowered the binoculars, thinking

about Maureen having to bail him out of jail, having been arrested as a Peeping Tom. Hell, he thought, and raised them again. He knew two things about Helen Ray. One, she used the equipment in her exercise room. Regularly. Two, she wasn't a natural blond.

At ten-fifteen Shanahan saw lights go off in several rooms and the porch light go on. Either she was expecting someone and getting the mood right or she was preparing to leave. The garage door went up and the little blue Miata, top on, backed out.

He couldn't be sure it was her, but who else could it be? For a moment he was torn. Should he follow her, or stay there and do his tricks in the house? Then he remembered that Howie Cross was watching Connell. And in Shanahan's mind, that's where she was heading.

She pulled out of the driveway, and Shanahan ducked the beam of her headlights coming in through the back of the van. He wished he'd brought Casey. He could be pretending to walk his dog, which people did in this neighborhood. They jogged, bicycled, and walked their dogs.

Shanahan, unfortunately, had no jogging outfit, no bicycle, and no dog at hand. He would chance it. He checked the views through front and side windows of the van, then the rear windows once more, and got out. Please, he thought, no nosy neighbors.

He looked at the the security sticker. "Thank you, Marty, for being so cheap." It didn't take long to pick the regular lock and only slightly longer to pick the dead bolt. Inside, the house was familiar to him. He had the tour earlier, thanks to Maureen, and he knew where he wanted to go. He didn't bother with the kitchen except for the small white wicker desk where she kept her papers and her list of phone numbers. If she had Connell's office phone, she must have his private number, because the one Shanahan had dialed earlier wasn't there. That didn't mean anything one way or another.

There was no basement. The washer and dryer were in a separate room and he found nothing unusual there. He checked what was obviously her bedroom, as well as the exercise room, with the Nautilus machine in a corner. Shanahan was pretty sure Marty didn't use it.

A strong woman, he thought, could easily have stabbed Samuel Puckett. Again he could not find the damning evidence he'd hoped for. He would have been surprised if he had.

In her bathroom he found a long blond hair curled around the stainless steel rim in the tub. It was worth the trip. When he came out, the two big cats stood in the hall, staring.

He looked out of the front window before he left. He could see his van. He could also see a pale blue car with a light on top, sitting behind it, headlights on the license plate.

Meridian Hills security, he thought. Shanahan waited. He counted to a hundred after the car drove off before he ventured out.

When he got back to the house, he went straight to the answering machine, despite Maureen telling him she'd been there all day and no one called. She was right, but he had pictured Howie Cross, outside a cheap motel at the public telephone, recounting how the lady in the blue Miata pulled up alongside the big Connell Mercedes and how the two of them went into the rooms.

Shanahan poured himself half a glass of J.W. Dant and sat on the sofa, clicking on the TV.

"You ready for court tomorrow?" Maureen asked, sitting beside him in her worn blue terry-cloth robe, her auburn hair wet with loose curls.

"No."

"How'd it go?"

"I don't know," he said, trying to lose himself in an inane conversation between Johnny Carson and some giggling starlet.

"It's a repeat, not that it makes much difference," Maureen said. "You prefer me to paddle my rear in the other room so you can think, or not think, whichever it is you're trying to do?"

Shanahan laughed, put his arm around her. "It's a puzzle, and it's not getting any clearer."

Almost simultaneously Casey gave his intruder bark and there was a muffled knock at the door.

Shanahan turned on the light, peered through the glass window and saw Howie Cross. He was bouncing up and down trying to keep warm, the lapels of his thin sports jacket turned up.

"Come in," Shanahan said, opening the door. Casey stopped barking, but sniffed at the man under the porch light, who had backed a few feet away, nearly falling down the steps.

"Let's talk out here," Cross said. "Okay?"

"He won't bite," Shanahan said.

"I've had gerbils attack me. It's all right out here. It won't take long to tell you the good news.

Shanahan stepped out into the cold, his breath materializing in front of his words. "Out with it, Howie. A blond lady in a blue Miata? Right?"

"Ummmm . . . no. Maybe this isn't such good news."

"What?"

"On Meridian Street around twenty-fifth, apartment 207, Sue Granelli." Howie Cross picked up quickly the fact that this wasn't the news Shanahan was waiting for. In a very small, encouraging voice, he continued. "Dark hair, pretty, very, very young. Maybe too young?"

"Well, it was a long shot."

"Wrong chick, huh?"

"Wrong chick, Howie." Shanahan laughed at the irony. S. Granelli was the girl Mr. Dunfy was cheating with. "But she's apparently doing all right for herself I thought I might have had it figured out. Helen was using Connell and his business to launder cocaine money, and banging him while she was at it. Then either Helen or Connell or the two of them together killed Puckett."

"Still could be," Howie said.

"One last chance maybe," Shanahan said, thinking about the hair samples Swann told him about and the strands of hair he had in his pocket. "Hey, you know, you are a little old to be called 'Howie'?"

"You like Howard the detective better?"

TWENTY-THREE

Shanahan had appeared at court cases before, though maybe only once or twice a year. And they were generally at the City-County Building, another tall glass box that housed the police department and holding cells, as well as municipal, criminal, and superior courts.

But he'd never seen it this way before. Outside was a bustle of reporters from newspapers throughout the state and from TV stations as far away as Fort Wayne. He counted fifteen TV and radio vans.

"You'd think Elvis was going to testify,"

he told Jennifer Bailey just inside the courtroom doors.

She looked up at him, a grimace on her face.

"Silvers was on all the local talk shows last week," she said, "saying a hell of a lot about street gangs and wild kids in the streets, despite the fact he said he couldn't say anything about this case in particular. I'm surprised he didn't grant an interview with the city apartment guide."

"Big show for such a short trial," Shanahan said, fully aware it would get under her skin. "So what do you want me to do when I take the stand?"

"Tell the truth. It's all we've got."

"Here's some truth. The police found the red Caddy."

"Oh, is there something pertinent I should know?" She moved to the desk beyond the seats and down to the left of the judge's bench, sure he would follow.

"They found strands of hair from several different people."

She stopped arranging her papers for a moment, stood and looked Shanahan square in the eye.

"You know, of course, I've ridden in that car."

"Yes, I would have guessed that."

"Are you going to play it my way?" she asked.

"For a while. But let's get beyond you right now."

She looked a little shocked for a moment, but only a moment. She gathered her composure quickly. "I guess that's fair."

"My guess is that if they want to talk about finding the car and the strands of hair, then it will be damaging to Leo and Billy. If they don't bring it up, maybe you should. A car was stolen, Ms. Bailey—maybe at the scene of the crime, maybe not—which means somebody else is involved in this besides the boys."

"Like most attorneys, Mr. Shanahan, I don't like to ask questions unless I know the answers."

"I'll try to get them for you. I'm not sure I'll have them when their expert witness on such things testifies, so you may have to set—"

"To set the stage. Okay. I can do that."

Maureen had found Tom English and was sitting with him. Next to him was Mai Lee. Shanahan approved. He sat with them. After the judge's remarks and instructions to the jury, Robert Silvers stood and began to speak.

"Today we have a grave matter before us. Today, we begin to determine the fate of our neighborhoods, the fates of our families and loved ones. Will our city streets be ruled as they are in cities such as Los Angeles, New York, and Detroit, or do we remain a city strong on family values, in fairness under the law?"

The judge, a white-haired lady who looked just a little tougher than most grandmothers, glared at the prosecutor. The opening statement was to show what the prosecution intended to prove, and it was more than obvious the handsome prosecutor was putting it in a favorable political context and asking for conviction on grounds other than evidence. Shanahan knew he wasn't impressing the judge, but what about the jury? What about the media? They'd certainly have some impressive sound bites.

Jennifer Bailey looked down at her papers.

"Today marks the beginning of that struggle. Seated at the table, dressed by the defense to look as if they are on their way to Sunday school, are Leonard Porter and

William Chatwin. William Chatwin, at the time of his arrest, we will show, wore a black tee-shirt with 'Megadeth,' emblazoned on the front. Megadeth," he repeated slowly, "not the clean, white starched shirt he wears today.

"But his crime and the crime of Leonard Porter went beyond attire. One of them plunged a bayonet into the heart of one of the city's finest policemen, a man devoted to protecting us from the scum who corrupt our children, rape our wives, and slink around in the night thieving and killing.

"William Chatwin and Leonard Porter not only brutally took the life of a fine human being, as we shall see, but robbed us, all of us," he let his gaze go over the entire jury box, "including the black community, robbing all of us of our protections against the likes of them.

"It is true, as I'm sure the defense will no doubt point out, there was no eyewitness to the heinous act itself, but we will show you, step by step, by expert testimony and modern technology, it could have been no one else."

Silvers enumerated each witness he intended to call and what they would prove, subtly interjecting racial guilt to the all-white jury.

"Make no mistake," Silvers concluded, "these are not poor little orphans who came to steal a few pennies to eat. William Chatwin and Leo Porter came fully prepared to kill, and kill they did."

From Shanahan's vantage point, Billy and Leo, both dressed in dark blue suits, remained quiet. Leo's shoulders were hunched, however. Billy seemed to almost recline in his seat, as if he were more amused than concerned, maybe watching a program on TV.

If Jennifer Bailey was concerned, she did not show it. She got up calmly and moved slowly and deliberately to the twelve jurors. She looked in each of their faces, fashioning a strange form of introduction with a smile and a nod.

"I'm Jennifer Bailey and I work for you. And it's clear after the opening statement that Mr. Robert Silvers will make a fine mayor of Indianapolis, but we must not allow the lives of two of the city's youths to be sacrificed at the altar of his political campaign."

"Objection." Silvers's co-counsel, a young black man, stood. There was a general rise in the chatter in the courtroom as reporters already had another sound bite for the six o'clock news.

"You know better than that," the judge said, smiling. "These are opening statements, Counselor. It seems to me defense has the same latitude as the prosecution. However, I would caution both counsels to limit the remainder of their time to the case at hand. You may proceed," she told Jennifer Bailey, who did not allow this early successful volley to show on her face.

"The heart of the prosecution's argument as outlined is centered on placing the boys at the scene of the crime." She looked at the jury, a moment before proceeding. "They were there. The prosecution will trot out a stream of expert testimony to prove that one or both robbed Samuel Puckett as he lay dead." She looked at the jury again allowing a significant pause. "Yes, they did that. We've said so from the beginning. I apologize for all of this tedious testimony taking up so much of your valuable time, but I urge you to be patient and I urge you to listen to the evidence, if there is any at all, that indicates it was Leo and Billy who committed the murder."

Jennifer Bailey walked back to the table, standing just so the jury could look at the two defendants.

"The prosecution correctly states there is no eyewitness to the heinous act. Yes, it was a heinous act, but the fact will remain at the end of this trial that there was no eyewitness to the murder. None. The prosecution will indicate that the defendants' fingerprints were found everywhere . . ." She paused. "Except on the murder weapon."

She raised her hands in a gesture that said this doesn't make sense.

"What you are asked to do here, prescribed by law, is not to decide whether you think they probably did it, or whether you believe they probably did it. 'Probably' is not enough in our system of justice. It requires you to consider their guilt with the words you've heard in every courthouse movie you've ever seen. You must be so convinced that these young boys killed this experienced policeman that you are prepared to say you believe it beyond any reasonable doubt.

"Reasonable doubt." She shook her head. "The prosecution cannot do it. But if Robert Silvers has his way, these boys will be painfully and cruelly executed, electrically shocked out of existence on evidence that proves only that they were engaged in a petty burglary attempt."

From there, the prosecution moved on immediately with their case, but without Robert Silvers, who passed back through the crowded courtroom with the assurance of a rock star, stealing—until the doors closed behind him—attention away from co-counsel, who was about to embark upon the nuts and bolts of the case.

The first to testify was the deputy coroner. He had a burr haircut and weighed possibly three hundred pounds. He sat confidently, spoke with care in a deep voice that gave him surprising authority. His weight, at first comic, gradually gave him presence, authority. He came across as knowledgeable and professional.

His testimony, in Shanahan's mind, was neither helpful nor harmful. After explaining the time of death and how that was determined, he had done little to advance anyone's knowledge. It had been simple. The victim had been stabbed with a bayonet entering the heart muscle with considerable force and causing immediate or near immediate death.

"Was it possible for the victim to have moved after he fell?" Jennifer Bailey asked on cross examination.

"Possible but not likely."

"Were there any other wounds, any indication that Samuel Puckett had attempted to defend himself?"

"No other wounds."

"Wouldn't you say that was pretty odd, considering he was an experienced police officer, attacked from the front?"

"That's out of my territory," he replied. She had, however, made her point, one Shanahan hoped she'd bring up again and again.

During the short ten-thirty recess, Shanahan talked to Jennifer, Billy and Leo. Billy said nothing. At first Shanahan thought he was bored. However, Billy was really distant, off in his heroic comic-book world where somehow the innocent were saved. Leo was hyper, his knees bouncing up and down nervously, biting so deep in a fingernail that blood appeared. He didn't acknowledge the pain. When Shanahan congratulated Jennifer Bailey on her opening statement, Leo joined in loudly.

"You got him, didn't you?" Leo said,

hanging on any strand of hope, however fragile.

"It's early. The hard part is coming up," she said softly.

Shanahan noticed Edie Porter in the back row, the only family of either of the boys to show up, and she was giving up a day's pay, two if she came back tomorrow.

He stopped by, said hello. She wore a black scarf over her head. "Is it raining outside?"

"What? Oh, the scarf, no my hair's a mess," she said. "How do you think it's going?"

"It looks good now, but it will no doubt have its peaks and valleys before it's over."

"What do you mean?"

"Just that sometimes you'll get encouraged and sometimes discouraged. Hang in there," he said.

What a thing to say: "Hang in there," Shanahan thought. Nobody would ever accuse him of being the sensitive, nurturing type.

Shanahan had a chance to explain to Tom English where everything stood, but wondered if Tom was going to be able to publish anything.

"It's awfully strange around there," he

said. "I had hoped it would get back to normal when Sarah came back, but she seems a lot different. Now that she owns the magazine, she's gotten so she doesn't want to rock the boat. I couldn't even tell her I was coming down. Weird."

The expert witness representing forensics was a thin man with a prominent nose and Adam's apple. He had wire glasses with thick lenses and a tiny, brittle voice.

Shanahan suspected this was the killer testimony, because Robert Silvers was back and asking the questions.

The forensics man had no presence at all, and Shanahan watched the jury. The same jury that had been magnetized by the deputy coroner who had very little to say was now tuned out. Some eyes were glazed. Some eyes darted about innattentively.

The forensics man spoke in emotionless tones and in technical jargon, which Silvers took great pains getting him to explain in terms the jury could understand. The witness was the kind of guy who would rather be in a lab coat in a room full of equipment than in a suit in a room full of curious people, but Silvers knew how to bring the attention back. He walked over by the jury box, looking at them, then at the witness as he asked questions. He stayed there long enough to reestablish a link with the jury, then moved back toward the docile man in the chair.

At first the forensics expert merely explained what both Shanahan and Jennifer Bailey knew were the facts and what would inevitably be brought out. Fingerprints putting Billy and Leo in the same room as the victim well within the time constraints established by the deputy prosecutor. He further stated that the blood on the shoes belonging to Leo Porter matched that of the victim, which was no surprise.

"Did you find footprints matching the sole of Leo Porter's shoes as well."

"Yes, we did."

"Did those footprints provide any other significant information?" Silvers looked back to the jury as if to say, pay special attention now.

"Most people trying to strike a downward blow would move to the ball of the foot at the moment of or slightly before impact to achieve more leverage. The depth of the wound indicated it was made with considerable force, and the footprint indicates that the ball of the foot had more weight on it than the heel of the shoe."

Jennifer Bailey began writing something, and Shanahan hoped that the nature of this current testimony wasn't causing her to change the plea. This was rough.

"Let me restate that for the jury. It is your expert opinion that this increased weight on the ball of the foot of Leo Porter's shoe indicates a natural weight shift that would occur during the stabbing of Samuel Puckett."

"It could, yes."

Jennifer Bailey continued to write on her lined yellow paper.

"And were there any other bloodied footprints at the scene of the crime?"

"None that we found."

Jennifer Bailey suddenly looked up as if she'd been struck herself.

"And you searched carefully?" Silvers asked.

"A team of four people were there for eight hours."

"Trained people?"

"Yes."

"Now just for the record, you also examined hundred-dollar bills that were in Billy and Leo's possession. Correct?"

"Yes."

"And you examined bills left in the victim's wallet?"

"Yes."

"And you examined bills that were in the possession of Mr. Price, owner of the liquor store?"

"Yes, I did."

"And did these bills have anything in common?"

"They were marked, and all contained fingerprints matching Leo Porter's."

"Thank you," Silvers said, then added while he glanced at the jury, "no further questions."

The judge, now stone-faced, called a two-hour recess. It was time for lunch, if anyone could eat.

TWENTY-FOUR

"Not now, Shanahan," Jennifer Bailey was pulling her papers together, looking harried. "I've got to think."

"No, you have to listen. Do you own a bathing suit?"

"Are you stark raving mad?"

"Answer." He said it so threateningly, he surprised himself.

"No, I don't, but what possible—"

"Have you ever been to Barbados?" Shanahan knew the answers to both questions, but he had to get her focused and he didn't particularly want her to know that he'd rifled her bureau drawers and examined her passport.

"Not in my life," she said angrily. "What are you doing?"

He took the photo from his pocket, the torn photo he'd found at Samuel Puckett's place. "You were never in this picture, were you?"

"No." Jennifer Bailey quieted. She looked at Shanahan expectantly. "I don't like the water, Mr. Shanahan, and I'm not particularly interested in the tanning effect of the sun. I saw that photograph the night I went to Sam's apartment, the night he died. I presumed that was his girlfriend's photo and he'd somehow dumped her from his life, and tearing her out of it was symbolic or something."

"I'm sure it was something, but I'm not sure he was the one who ripped out the other person.

"If it were someone else, and I say 'if,'

then they would have had to have gotten there quickly. I went to his apartment as soon as I learned he was killed. Not very flattering, I suppose, to be more concerned with my career than his death, but that's the way it was. They hadn't even identified the body yet, but they showed the stakeout house and I knew it was him. Who else . . . ?"

"The murderer was the first to know," Shanahan said.

"And we're back to the same question. Who is the murderer?"

"I may know. You have to ask the question about the car, about the hair samples. Promise?"

Lieutenant Swann was in his office. He sat behind a cheap desk, with all the papers and desk accessories neatly arranged. He had a large mug of coffee before him that said WORLD'S GREATEST DAD, and a picture of a woman and two not quite teenage daughters, presumably the donors of his coffee cup.

"What about the hair?"

Swann shrugged. "They don't tell me."

"Can you match this?" Shanahan tossed

the envelope down in front of Lieutenant Swann.

Swann opened the envelope, pulled out a strand of long, blond hair.

"Who's the owner?"

"I'll tell you if it matches," Shanahan said, not wanting to explain how he came by it.

"Helen Ray's? Right?" Swann waited for an answer but didn't get it. "Okay, Mr. Detective. It's a long shot. If I took bets, I'd take this one and give you big odds."

"Why are you so sure?"

"The car wasn't at the scene of the crime. He didn't drive his own car to an undercover house."

"But if the murderer knew him intimately and well, she would know what kind of car he had and where to find it."

"A she? You have it narrowed down to a she? Helen Ray. She's a bimbo, Shanahan. I hate that word, but it describes her. She'd never be able to cover her tracks. I talked with her, Shanahan. She's not that smart. But I will . . . I will do this for you so you'll finally give it up. Okay?"

"Okay," Shanahan said. "When?"

"Court in recess?"

"Yeah."

"I'll see if I can have it by the end of the day. No promises. But I will do my best."

"Mr. Roberts, you testified that the pressure on the ball of the foot was consistent with the striking of a fatal blow. Is that correct?" Jennifer Bailey stood in front of the forensics expert.

"Yes."

"Could it be consistent with someone down on their haunches in order to remove a billfold from the body of the victim?"

"Yes."

"So your testimony was not meant to be conclusive?" She did as Silvers had done, looked back to the jury.

"No."

"I see. This footprint in question was the only one found next to the body, actually the only one in the room, and the prosecution suggests this is the footprint exacted at the time the murderer struck the blow. Perhaps you can tell me how the blood was there to be stepped in before the blow was struck?"

So simple; you can't step in the blood of the victim *before* he's a victim. The prosecution goofed. The footprint only established Billy and Leo's presence, not their guilt. And Bailey had already admitted the kids were there. Shanahan breathed a sign of relief. Even he didn't catch the obvious contradiction.

"Perhaps it is as you suggest," the forensics man said calmly. "The footprint was the result of someone bending over the body and removing a wallet or something."

"Perhaps," she said.

"And there were no other marks on the floor or in the blood on the floor?"

"Marks?"

"Yes, marks. Was it just a smooth-surfaced pool of blood on the floor?" Jennifer asked, then added, "I saw the photographs."

"There was an indication that the deceased may have moved before he became deceased or that he was moved after he became deceased, but only a few inches and that pattern was visible. Yes, if you call that a mark."

"Perhaps the body was moved to erase another pair of footprints?"

"That would be conjecture," he said.

"Wouldn't it be conjecture to say that wasn't the case?"

"I suppose." Mr. Roberts looked even

more uncomfortable. He looked at Robert Silvers. Silvers did not return the glance.

There was the ring of victory in her voice as she continued. "Perhaps you could tell me why there would be fingerprints on the windowsill, on the doorknobs, on the walls, and none on the murder weapon. There were none on the murder weapon, am I right?"

"No, you're not right," he trounced, taking perhaps a little too much joy in correcting her. "There were prints on the weapon, we simply could not identify them. You see, the handle of the bayonet had two types of ridges, one spiraling down"—the judge handed him the bayonet, a tag dangling from it—"like this. The rest of the handle is cross-hatched. Raised cross-hatching to make the grip surer. Unfortunately, it means we only get pieces of prints, wholly inconclusive."

Jennifer Bailey turned and glared at Robert Silvers. Apparently he'd misled her. Part of her argument had just leaped out of the window.

"You were asked to look into the matter of Mr. Puckett's car, were you not?"

"Yes, I was."

"And what was the nature of the investigation?"

"To examine particles of hair to determine if they belonged to either or both of the defendants."

"What were your conclusions?"

"They did not."

"So it's likely that someone else drove the car, that is, someone or someone besides the defendants."

"All it means," he said, head raised and glancing down at her, "is that we did not find strands of the defendants' hair."

"The room was covered with blood, was it not?"

"It does not rule out the possibility the defendants were in the automobile," he continued.

"I'm asking you about blood now, Mr. Roberts. Please answer the questions in the order that I ask them."

"The room in which the death occurred had blood on the floor and some on the walls, if that's what you're asking."

"Yes. And on the ceiling, is that not correct?"

"Some."

"So, there must have been a pretty incredible eruption of blood to cause that much blood to get on the ceiling."

"Yes, that's true."

"And would you not expect that the blood would also have gotten on the murderer in such a case?"

"That depends on a lot of things," the forensics expert said. "Certainly it could have."

"Just could? Wouldn't that be likely?"

"I'm not qualified to make book in a criminal investigation, Mrs. Bailey."

"Thank you, that will be all." She looked at Shanahan, and it didn't take a telepathic to understand her message. It was, "You better come up with something."

Mr. Price testified next. He established the boys near the scene of the crime before and after it occurred. He also confirmed the passing of the marked bills, claiming the boys did have ID's.

Jennifer Bailey played the tape of the transaction, which clearly put Price in jeopardy for selling to minors, but did little to advance the case, except to make note of the clothing—that Billy Chatwin had indeed worn the same clothes before and after the crime. Had Price noticed blood on his clothes? He'd didn't "recollect" he did.

Shanahan and Maureen were on the stand only briefly, and it was clear they were there to show Billy's willingness to brandish a gun.

Lieutenant Swann's testimony not only established the red Caddy as irrelevant, since it was apparently and coincidentally stolen from Puckett's apartment garage—not from the scene of the crime—but went on to reinforce all the links the prosecution had made so far. Silvers had used Swann as summation, to restate every piece of evidence one more time.

And though there should have been logical doubts, at least shadows of doubts, Shanahan knew Swann's simple presentation was a blockbuster. It boiled down to: If it wasn't them, who was it? Could there be even a hint in the jury's minds that it could have been someone else? By now there wasn't.

Besides that, Swann came across as smart, professional, sincere, and, worst of all, convinced of the boys' guilt.

The judge called it a day. Defense could pick up on the cross-examination of Swann tomorrow morning. She could present her witnesses if she had any, and they might even be able to send the case to the jury before the end of the day.

Shanahan followed Swann to the police wing, then up to the lab.

"I want to show you, so you'll never have a doubt," Swann said. "Look." Shanahan placed his eyes over the microscope. "No fancy testing needed. These hairs did not come from the same person. As I told you, the bimbo isn't connected."

"You're sure?" Shanahan asked. However, he knew Swann was right.

"We did the fancy testing. No match."

"Where's the other hair you found?"

"Here," Swann said, nudging over a Ziploc baggie.

"Can I touch?"

"Sure," Swann said.

Shanahan slipped each of the three remaining hairs on the little glass plate.

"One is probably Puckett's. And the rest? Well, Puckett was a good cop, but he was a ladies' man. He got a real kick out of having to spend so much time at Sweethearts. Ladies, Shanahan. But it isn't the bimbo."

"This one hair looks strange," Shanahan said. "Look."

"You mean the short one on the left, the straight black one. It's just a woman who dyes her hair. Get the gray out. As I said, a ladies' man."

Shanahan returned to the courtroom to pick up Maureen. She was still talking with Tom English. Jennifer Bailey was still at the defendants' table, though Billy and Leo were gone. Beside her was Robert Silvers. Silvers was doing the talking.

"Now's the time to change your party affiliation, Jennifer. An attractive black woman in our party. You could write your own ticket. . . ."

Shanahan noticed she met his questioning gaze directly, but she said nothing. Whether that had something to do with his own approach, he wasn't sure.

Up close, Silvers had larger-than-life features, large nose, large eyes, big mouth with a lot of teeth. As in theater, this look, handsome at a distance with exaggerated features, stood him well in speech making and also gave him power up close. Charisma.

"I think I can prove their innocence," Shanahan said to Jennifer Bailey.

Silvers looked startled, but only for a split second, then his face relaxed into a big smile.

"Good thing you're not on the jury," he said.

Jennifer looked at Silvers, then back at Shanahan. "Let's go talk," she said, with a look that admonished Shanahan for saying so much in front of Silvers. Shanahan smiled back. He wouldn't have missed that brief break in the mask for anything, and he liked the idea of putting the powerful man on edge.

"Who is this guy?" Silvers asked, appearing to be lighthearted.

"A voter," Jennifer Bailey said.

"Well, I'll see you tomorrow morning," Silvers said, nodding to Jennifer and casting a glance at Shanahan. "Think about our talk, Jennifer. It's the right time in your career."

"What was that all about?" Jennifer asked when Silvers was out of earshot. "Helen Ray?"

"Helen Ray is a bust, at least for the moment. But there is a possibility that one of James Connell's hairs found its way into Sam Puckett's red Caddy."

"James Connell . . . the James Connell of whatever, whatever and whatever, big business Connell? You're trying to tell me this man who's on more foundation letterheads than the mayor killed Sam and stole his automobile, for heaven's sake? Are you . . . ?"

"Crazy? Senile?"

Shanahan realized he'd never brought the Connell name up in Jennifer Bailey's presence before—for good reason.

"I'm sorry. You've accused me, Helen Ray, and now somebody who may be an asshole, but hardly so stupid as get involved with undercover cops, stabbings, drugs, go-go girls, and stolen cars."

"I didn't accuse you, but you have to admit you've got a pretty strange connection with undercover cops yourself?"

"Yes, but what on earth could be the motive?" she asked, incredulous, then surprisingly supplied a motive. "Money laundering?"

"Could be. I don't know."

"There's a positive ID on the hair?"

"Uh . . . no. Not exactly." If Shanahan had her convinced of the possibility, he knew he was about to un-convince her. "Connell dyes his hair. The sample the police found shows a strand of dyed hair."

"That's it? There's probably fifty thousand people in this city who dye their hair.

Besides, you were so convinced it was a woman of color."

"That's true," Shanahan said. He knew he was on thin ice, and she made it pretty clear for him just how thin it was. "However, Connell was pretty eager to see the kids fry. He even took over the magazine to get at them."

"He's of the same political persuasian as Robert Silvers. That's no surprise. So is sixty percent of the white population in the state of Indiana."

What he had done, Shanahan now realized, was completely demoralize her. The defense wasn't going well, and here was this ancient, crackpot detective reaching into thin air for a guilty party to get them off.

He knew better than to say anything more about his suspect. "I'm sorry. Try to concentrate on tomorrow."

Shanahan asked English to go back to the magazine offices and search for a strand of James Connell's hair.

Now it was Tom English's turn to think Shanahan was loony.

"What?"

"No way," Maureen said. "It was a woman, I tell you."

TWENTY-FIVE

Tom English had failed to find a sample of Connell's hair in his office. He'd told Shanahan that the night before, when he phoned, told him that he'd gone over the upholstery of the chair and the carpet with a flashlight and magnifying glass.

It had been a long shot, Shanahan told himself as the early morning light cast the bedroom in a dreary gray. Maureen was still asleep, the sheet not quite over her freckled shoulders, her hair half hiding her face. On the nightstand beside her was the clock radio, the electric blue digits just switching from 5:58 to 5:59.

He crept out of bed, put on the coffee, showered, and debated for a moment whether he'd put on a suit to confront James Connell and decided jeans and a sweater would be more comfortable. He wasn't testifying today.

Shanahan took his cup of coffee out the back door and tossed the tennis ball for Casey, who swept down the lawn and into the lily stalks to retrieve it. Too early yet for the stray sounds of the neighborhood; the morning was quiet and smelled of autumn. Soon the ancient maple would turn a yellow gold and the hard maple behind his fence, in the neighbor's yard, would turn a purplish red.

Shanahan tossed the ball again. He was oddly calm, the calm that comes from those momentary recognitions that life and death unfolds as it should, that he would do now what he could, and if that failed, so be it.

It would take an hour, maybe forty-five minutes, to get to the Connell estate. He looked at his watch: 6:33 A.M. He called Casey into the house, went into the bedroom, kissed Maureen, went out the front door and got into his car.

He took a deep breath.

Shanahan had to wait at least fifteen minutes at the gate. A woman's voice had told him "just a moment" after when he spoke through the box and gave his name.

The extraordinary, rolling green front lawn was now dappled with sunlight as he drove through the gate and up the long blacktop drive. The huge home looked like it belonged to a university or country club, and the woman who had directed him down to the pottery shed on his first visit stood at the front door.

"Mr. Shanahan . . . uh, thank you, Maribel . . ." Connell emerged and dismissed her. "Mr. Shanahan, I was sure we concluded our business when we met at the office."

He was dressed in a gray suit, blue shirt and paisley tie, very much the way he had dressed at the office. He stood in the doorway, his arm leaning against the doorjamb as if for comfort, but in effect it barred Shanahan's entry.

"Police have discovered an unusual strand of hair in Sam Puckett's automobile."

"Who is Sam Puckett and of what possible concern could that be to me?"

"It was a gray hair, dyed black." Shanahan's gaze went to Connell's hairline, then to Connell's eyes.

Connell grinned, a condescending smile that seemed to come naturally. "With all due respect, Mr. Shanahan, I've endured quite enough of this foolishness. I'm a patient man, and I can only believe that this farfetched idea you have that I'm involved in some shady, backstreet criminal activity is the result of some senior citizen aberration on your part. If you are indeed a licensed investigator, I'm sure that there are agencies that govern such licenses and have criteria for keeping them. Is that clear?"

"You dye your hair, Mr. Connell?"

"What I'm trying to tell you, if you're sane enough to understand, is that I'm not the kind of guy you want to fuck with."

"There was also a silver-blond hair, longer, found in the automobile as well."

"I have called the police. And I will make a complaint. If you choose to remain here, I shall have you forcibly removed. Your choice."

"I guess the lives of two no-account kids is a small sacrifice to maintain your reputation in the community."

Connell looked up and over Shanahan's shoulder. Shanahan turned to see a tan sedan, an unmarked police car curling up the long drive.

"Too late," Connell said. He shook his head. "A man your age should be enjoying his leisure, Mr. Shanahan. A little trailer court in Fort Lauderdale, maybe."

Shanahan was surprised to see Lieutenant Swann get out of the car. He was with another plainclothesman.

"Mr. Connell, Mr. Shanahan," Swann

said, then to Connell, "I'm Lieutenant Swann, Homicide."

"Homicide?" Connell smiled uneasily.

"Well, I was out this way on a case and I overheard the call, so I just came on over."

"Whatever," Connell said. "I'm afraid that this gentleman has the craziest notion that I'm involved in some murder downtown and is harassing me and my wife with this bizarre notion."

"Hmmm, is that true, Mr. Shanahan?"

"I've talked with Mrs. Connell once, a pleasant, unstrained conversation that occurred because she thought I was here to pick up her pottery. I visited Mr. Connell once at his office, and now this. I'd hardly call it harrassment."

"Mr. Shanahan, I don't have to tell you that Mr. Connell has done an awful lot for this city. And he is hardly the type to put a bayonet in the chest of a policeman. What on earth would make you think this about him?"

It occurred to Shanahan that Swann wasn't there by accident. He'd no doubt been tailed. Why? At Silvers's request? Undoubtedly.

"Aren't you testifying this morning?" Shanahan asked.

"The trial's been postponed until this afternoon. Something's come up." Swann's eyes connected with Shanahan's, and Shanahan could decipher that ever so slight smile on Swann's thin lips. It was saying "go for it."

Shanahan pulled the half-torn photograph from his pocket and handed it to Swann.

"Um-hum, that's Puckett. He seems to be enjoying himself. Who's missing?" He handed the photo to Mr. Connell.

"Mrs. Connell," Shanahan said.

"That's preposterous," Connell said. "Do I have to listen to this?"

"No, you don't," Lieutenant Swann said. "You can go back in, if you like. Shanahan and I will clear up this little matter."

When Connell stayed, Swann looked at Shanahan and winked.

"Now if we knew that to be a fact, what would that prove?"

"Puckett and Mrs. Connell were having an affair."

"This is ludicrous," Connell said.

"Let's humor him," Swann said, "then we can put all this behind us and finish our prosecution of those two teenage murderers we have in custody. Go on, Shanahan."

"If you match the hairs you retrieved from Sam Puckett's car, you'll find they match Mr. Connell and Mrs. Connell. We can clear this up real fast if the Connells will part with a couple of samples."

"No," came a voice behind Connell. Mrs. Connell forged her way between her husband and the door. She plucked the torn photograph from her husband's grasp. "You're very good, Mr. Shanahan, but I helped you out when I talked about sailing, didn't I?"

"Yes, but I didn't catch it right away. I was sure it was someone else with Puckett. You met in Barbados?"

"Yes," she said.

"Mrs. Connell, you have the right to remain—"

"I know, I know," she interrupted, brushing the concern aside. "It was so funny meeting someone half a world away, someone you couldn't possibly have met in your own city, though he lived there too." She smiled and continued to talk with Shanahan as if the others weren't present. "You know—and I know you know, you're a wise man—even when you're older and someone young and handsome like Sam takes an interest in you and you're on this fantasy island anyway, it's so easy to believe that it's fate or something that you met. We both loved sailing and . . . what can I say? It wasn't supposed to end. I wasn't about to let it."

"Please don't say any more," Connell said.

"I killed him. I went there to get him back or kill him. Simple as that. He didn't know me well enough, after all. He laughed when I pulled out the bayonet. He laughed when I raised it over him. He looked so surprised when it went in."

She spoke clearly and dry-eyed.

"I was a bloody mess," she said, "my clothes, my hair. I found a jacket, some jeans and a hat. I put them on over my clothing and I left."

"How did you leave?" Shanahan asked.

"I'd driven to the Hilton downtown and I took a taxi from there. So I didn't have my car. I walked down the street, looking for a telephone booth to call Jimmy. He picked me up. I told him what happened, and he said he'd take care of it. I gave him the key to Sam's place because he wanted to remove the cards I'd sent Sam and anything else that would link us together. Jimmy," she said to Mr. Connell, "you should have taken the whole photograph. You're just not awfully bright sometimes."

"Why were you following me?" Shanahan asked Swann as they waited for Mrs. Connell to gather some belongings.

"It was Silvers's idea. He said you told him they were innocent and could prove it. He didn't believe it, thought you were out there somewhere in the twilight zone, but it made him nervous. He's not the kind of guy who takes chances, especially when his career is on the line. If there was proof he wanted to be the one to uncover it. He didn't want some sort of Perry Mason finish, where the prosecutor ends up with egg on his face. Not in an election year, especially."

"Well, thanks for coming by," Shanahan said.

"My pleasure," Swann said. "I do like to see justice done and the system work."

"The system worked?" Shanahan said.

"In its usual way. Remember, I told you it wasn't Helen Ray."

"So what about the Rays, Lieutenant Swann?"

"The system may take a little longer in that case. It's Detroit. A little bomb in Indy won't be top priority for them, and without them, we can't do much."

Mrs. Connell came out of the house. Her hair, that strange mix of silver, blond, and gold, was swept back in an elegant bun. Her Barbados-tanned, weather-lined face seemed neither nervous nor afraid.

"Were you going to let the kids go to the chair?" Shanahan asked her.

"I don't know, Mr. Shanahan, I hope not." She looked at her husband. His face was frozen, as untelling as stone.

"You suppose I could get that Mrs. Bailey to defend me?" she said, smiling, knowing full well what she was asking.

"I don't know that it's a good idea," Shanahan said.

"She is a pretty woman. Tell her I'm sorry."

The evening paper carried a front-page, above-the-fold story. There was a quarter-page photograph of Prosecutor Silvers behind a gaggle of microphones. The caption read: "Prosecutor says 'system works,' credits his office and the police department for tenacity in Puckett murder case."

Shanahan threw down the paper. He went to the telephone and dialed the

Dunfys. Mrs. Dunfy answered, and Shanahan asked for her husband.

"Tell your attorney to stop sending me letters," Shanahan told him. "I get enough junk mail from funeral homes and cemeteries."

"You're a smartass, and you'll pay," Mr. Dunfy said.

"You're a hypocrite, and you'll pay if you don't stop the letters. Ms. Granelli on Meridian Street is a very lovely young prostitute with many wealthy and influential clients, including a Mr. Connell, who's now up as accessory to a murder. Do you really want all this dragged out in court?"

There was silence on the other end.

"Dunfy?"

"No. I don't." Dunfy's voice was very small, like a little boy whose bluff was called and was about to get a whipping.

"We're all little kids, aren't we, Mr. Dunfy?"

"We have some mail," Maureen said, her words fighting a sudden upsurge of wind coming off the bay.

"Don't open it," he said, carefully stepping over the black lava rocks, finally getting his footing on the sandy beach.

"It's from Tom."

"English?"

She opened the large manila envelope and pulled out a newspaper. Clipped to the front page was a letter.

Guys, some things to report. I left *Metro Monthly* and started to work on an alternative newspaper called *The New Times.* The pay is terrible, but they liked the story on Billy and Leo (see newspaper). Seems as if Sarah Mundy got the magazine, not because she knew about the murder or James Connell's womanizing, but because he'd written an agreement out years ago with a Magic Marker on a pair of her panties and she never washed them. Sarah Mundy's panties—it boggles the mind. Billy and Leo have been released in the custody of a cop. Lieutenant Charles Rafferty. He says he knows you. Says if I see you, to say hi from him and Edie Porter. According to Mai Lee, Helen Ray left Marty and moved to Detroit, leaving him in shaky control of Sweethearts where strange characters from Detroit are hanging around. Mai Lee now works at a downtown club. She likes it a lot better. Oh, one final word. Mai Lee and I stopped at that bar you told me about. Delaney's. Never again. All I did was order a frozen daiquiri, and the guy went off on some tirade screaming about ferns and brunches. What was that all about? Anyway, have a good time in Hawaii. Mai Lee says hi too.

Shanahan handed the letter to Maureen and flipped through the pages of *New Times* until he found the story by Tom English:

Nobody seemed to have known much about Leo Porter and William Chatwin. Nobody seemed to have cared much either. But nearly everyone believed that one of them stabbed a policeman while the other watched. It was all that simple. They were nabbed and the investigation officially closed twenty four hours after the crime was committed. The city's prosecutor says that the youths' final vindication is proof that "the system" works.

The facts indicate otherwise. Will

we feel so comfortable when we know them . . .

Shanahan sat down on the sand, the tide rolling in on his feet. He looked up at the clear blue skies and the rolling green hills of Maui on the other side of the bay and thought how wonderful it was. Two more weeks in paradise with a happy, beautiful woman.

He read the rest of Tom English's story as a gentle breeze rattled the pages.